THE LADY OF A GRUMP

THE LADIES OF THE ARISTOCRACY

LINDA RAE SANDE

Twisted Teacup
PUBLISHING

The Secrets of a Viscount

The Widowers of the Aristocracy

The Dream of a Duchess

The Vision of a Viscountess

The Conundrum of a Clerk

The Charity of a Viscount

The Cousins of the Aristocracy

The Promise of a Gentleman

The Pride of a Gentleman

The Holidays of the Aristocracy

The Christmas of a Countess

The Knot of a Knight

The Heirs of the Aristocracy

The Angel of an Astronomer

The Puzzle of a Bastard

The Choice of a Cavalier

The Bargain of a Baroness

The Jewel of an Earl's Heir

The Vixen of a Viscount

The Honor of an Heir

The Ladies of the Aristocracy

The Lady of a Grump

Beyond the Aristocracy

The Pleasure of a Pirate

The Making of a Mistress

The Lyon's Den (Dragonblade Publishing)

The Courage of a Lyon

Stella of Akrotiri

Origins

Deminon

Diana

CHAPTER 1

A FAREWELL AND A
DEPARTURE

ecember 1837, the London docks

Thomas Grayson, Marquess of Billingsley, regarded his mother with a look of worry. "I can delay the trip, Mother. I don't have to go."

Lady Patience Billingsley placed a black kid-gloved hand on her son's arm. "You will go. We've been planning your Grand Tour for over a year. I'll not let your father's death interfere," she insisted, doing her best not to cry over her only son's impending departure. "His man of business has sent a letter to the Lord Chancellor on your behalf. When you return, you'll be recognized as his heir and take your seat in the House of Lords."

Nodding, Thomas jerked when a boatswain's whistle sounded from the deck of the *Fairweather*. His valet, Rogers, was waiting to go on board the three-masted sailing ship, his hands clutching the handles of two valises. Thomas' trunk had been loaded earlier that morning. "I'll write when I arrive in Naples," he promised.

"Your cicerone knows when to expect your arrival. He'll meet you at the docks," Patience said, referring to the Italian who would be Thomas' guide for his trip through the Kingdom of the Two Sicilies. "In his latest note, he said he would have the contacts you'll need for when you get to Greece," she explained, holding out a folded letter. "Do you have your money?"

Thomas accepted the missive and tucked it into an inside pocket of his great coat. "Yes, yes, Mother. And Rogers has some, too. Thought it best we not keep it all in one place."

The reminder of money had him glancing about nervously, as if he expected a pickpocket to rob him. Despite the chill in the air—it had snowed earlier that morning and gray clouds still hung over Wapping—the docks were crowded with passengers, porters, dock-workers and those who were sending loved ones off on trips to Europe and beyond.

"That's very wise of you," Patience replied, her gaze darting to the Thames.

The dark brown water beneath the gangway was as cloudy as the skies above, and from the way it moved, she knew the *Fairweather* would need to depart soon.

With the reality of her son's impending leave setting in, Patience knew if she didn't get back to her town coach, she would burst into tears at any moment.

"Now, go find your cabin. You're due to set sail at any moment."

Thomas leaned over and kissed her on the cheek. "Are you quite sure you'll be all right?"

A smile replaced Patience's look of worry. "As soon as you're off, I am as well."

"What's this?" he asked, turning once again to face her.

"I'm going to Grayson Park," she replied, referring to the Billingsley country estate in southern Shropshire. "Spend the winter there and probably the spring and summer, too, so be sure to write to me there."

Thomas furrowed his dark brows. "All by yourself?" he asked.

He looked so much like his father when he displayed the expression that could be annoyance, disbelief, or concern, Patience nearly winced. It would serve him well as a marquess, as it probably did his father, but Patience was able to hide the reason for her immediate reaction.

Disgust.

By the time David Grayson, the sixth Marquess of Billingsley, had died, she had grown to dislike the marquess. Intensely. Their unexpected marriage had not been a love match. Despite her mother's assurance that she would one day grow to love the man, the best Patience could manage was a grudging respect—once she had overcome her fear of the older man. She couldn't understand how her father, Robert Seward,

Earl of Eversham, could even claim to be friends with such a disagreeable sort.

When she learned that there had been little in the way of a dowry available when it came to her—Patience was the youngest of four daughters—she understood her father's motivation.

Billingsley wanted her, and he didn't care that her dowry was a paltry thousand pounds.

After learning the marquess kept a string of mistresses and made no attempt to hide the fact, Patience had resigned herself to finding joy in other aspects of her life in the aristocracy. The Season's entertainments filled most of those days and nights, and the rest of the year, she attended the theatre and took tea with other ladies in their parlors or in hers.

Now she merely wished for solitude. A bit of time away from London to do what she wished and when. Once Thomas was on his way to Naples, she would have her driver stop by the townhouse to collect her trunks, and they would be on their way to Grayson Park.

"With your lady's maid, I hope?" Thomas added, interrupting her reverie.

"Oh, no. I'm leaving Baxter. Or rather, she is leaving me. She gave notice last week," Patience explained. "She's decided to retire from service. It's perfect timing, really."

Thomas' eyes rounded. "What will you do?"

Patience nearly laughed at hearing the concern in

his query, as if he thought her incapable of dressing herself or seeing to her own hair. "I'll simply hire another once I'm at Grayson Park," she replied with a shrug. "I'll be fine, Thomas. Now get on board before you're left behind," she said with a *shooing* motion.

He kissed her on the cheek one last time, gave a bow, and joined his valet on the gangway.

Patience grinned in the morning light and did her best to keep her tears at bay. The temptation to beg him to stay had been almost too much, and she knew he would have delayed his trip had she made any sound of protest.

When he and Rogers disappeared, Patience hurried off to where her driver, Jeffrey Styles, stood next to the Billingsley town coach. He opened the door for her and helped her in. "The townhouse, my lady?"

"Yes, Styles. Buchanan said the traveling coach would be ready when we arrive," she said, referring to the Grayson townhouse butler. "Are you packed?"

"I am, my lady," Styles replied, giving her an enthusiastic nod.

"You don't mind living in the country for a few months?" She had discussed the issue with Buchanan, thinking the butler would have to hire a different driver to take her to Grayson Park since she wanted to keep the equipage once she arrived. With Derbyshire so close, she thought occasional jaunts through the Peak District would provide opportunities to draw or paint. Mayhap visit a country house or two.

"Not at all, my lady. I'm looking forward to getting out of the city again," he replied. "And I already know the Grayson Park staff, of course."

From his comment, Patience was reminded that Styles had been to Grayson Park in the past. Several times. Sometimes it was to take her and Billingsley for the summer months. She was quite sure one of her husband's mistresses had ridden with him on occasion —the times when he would announce he was leaving for the country without having given her any sort of notice, and then he would be gone for weeks at a time.

Perhaps Styles had formed an attachment with a servant or a housemaid during his prior visits. The thought had Patience displaying a wan grin as she made her way into the Georgian townhouse.

Seeing her reflection in the cheval mirror in her bedchamber, Patience winced. Despite her black hair and fair complexion, the black bombazine walking mourning gown, its hem and piping done in black crepe, looked positively hideous on her. The jet decorations centering the black crepe rosettes that lined the half-sleeves and high standing collar did nothing to enhance the gown. Worse, the matching Claremont bonnet did little to improve her appearance. At least its black crepe and sarcenet brim was lined in double white crepe. Had it been all black, she might have tossed it into the fireplace.

Widows weeds. Patience shuddered at the thought she should wear them for six months before moving to lavender for half-mourning. Once she was in Shropshire, she had every intention of packing them away in a trunk and having them taken to the attic.

Anxious to be done with London, Patience took one last look through the Westminster townhouse before she climbed into the Billingsley traveling coach. Although its ebony exterior had been recently polished, its age was apparent, and the gold-painted seal of the Billingsley marquessate had been covered with a layer of black paint.

Instead of having the faded seal touched up or completely redone, she had ordered Buchanan to have it painted over earlier that morning. Riding in an unmarked coach for three or four days would no doubt be safer than advertising the fact that a marquess or marchioness was ensconced within.

She was reminded of her son's steps to protect his blunt and knew she had made the right decision.

"Be careful, my lady," Styles warned as she stepped into the equipage. "The paint is still a bit damp."

"I will, Mr. Styles," she replied. "Even if it's covered in dust by sunset, I won't mind."

Jeffrey seemed to think on the matter for a few seconds before he said, "More like mud, my lady, given the snow that fell last night."

Patience grinned, already feeling lighter. "Either way, I shan't mind," she claimed.

A moment after she had settled in the sky blue velvet squabs in the direction of travel, she pulled a quilt over her lap against the December chill. She watched through the glass window as Styles and one of the grooms completed their check of the coach and the matched Cleveland bays. A slight jerk told her the driver had climbed onto his seat.

Once they were in motion, she opened a gothic novel and within minutes, she was lost in its story.

CHAPTER 2
AN EARL RECEIVES NEWS

eanwhile, at Higgins House in the very southern tip of Staffordshire Maxwell Higgins, seventh Earl of Greenley, downed the rest of his glass of brandy and cursed as he attempted to read his correspondence. Holding out the parchment as far as he could from his face, he closed first one eye and then the other in an effort to bring the even, feminine script into focus.

Why couldn't his oldest sister, Barbara, write using larger letters, he wondered as he finally gave up and searched about the large oak desk for his pair of reading glasses. Finding them beneath the latest report from his man of business in London, he cursed again when he remembered he owed the solicitor some answers to his latest queries involving the earldom's holdings.

Writing that letter would have to wait. He had no patience for putting into words what he knew in his head. Despite his having devoted his adult life to bringing the Greenley earldom back from the brink of bankruptcy, the assets he had managed to acquire were by no means large nor particularly valuable. To have to list them all seemed unproductive, especially when it was the land of the earldom that paid most of the bills. Well, and some sheep.

Setting the wire-rimmed spectacles on the end of his nose, he leaned back and read the missive.

Life seemed charmed for Barbara Higgins Slater these days. He knew it hadn't always been—Father's fault, not his—but she was married to the love of her life, had two grown sons to show for it, and was enjoying her lot as a countess and as the mistress of Ellsworth Park in Oxfordshire. At some point in the next decade or so, she would be the Marchioness of Devonfield.

Well, folderol, he thought as he crumpled the letter into a ball and tossed it into the stone fireplace. Before he had a chance to think twice and rescue it from its fate, flames quickly consumed it. "Dammit," he whispered.

"Will you require anything else this evening, my lord?" Bertram asked from the threshold of the earl's study.

Max turned to regard his butler with a frown—his usual expression. "No. Go to bed. I've some more correspondence to get through, and then I'll turn in."

Hesitant to say much more at this time of the

evening—the later it was, the more easily irritated his master became—Bertram nodded. "Very good, sir. I'll leave the lights on in the corridor upstairs," he offered, secretly glad his curmudgeon of a master had paid to retrofit Higgins House for gas lighting the year before.

Although the earl had grumbled about the cost, complained about the inconvenience when the workmen were there installing the lines, and then balked at the realization he would have to pay for the gas going forward, Bertram had reminded him they would no longer have to purchase candles.

Somewhat appeased, Max had then mentioned he preferred candlelight to gaslight.

Bertram knew not to reply. There was no pleasing the Earl of Greenley. There hadn't been a way to please the "Earl of Grump" in the fifteen years Bertram had been a butler at Higgins House.

At least the latest cook had agreed to stay on once she was assured she wouldn't have to speak with the earl. As the wife of the Higgins House groom and a decent cook when it came to preparing the meals for his lordship and the servants, Mrs. Cruthers maintained a pleasant demeanor and didn't humiliate the scullery maid when she made a mistake.

Fearful of the earl's wrath, the two housemaids who saw to the country manor house—Janet Ludlow and Agnes Sherman—were good about staying hidden whilst they worked, sneaking into the study to do their chores when their master was off to Kidderminster on business and tidying the master suite when his lordship went for his daily horseback ride.

The single footman, Fields, seemed immune to the earl's insults, as if he'd grown up with them and knew not to take them personally.

The laundress was so good about remaining hidden, Bertram sometimes wondered if she had left their employ, so he was always surprised when the week's laundry would appear in neat folded piles at the end of everyone's beds, ready to be put away.

Bertram might have quit his master years ago and moved on to a different country house, but Maxwell Higgins knew his bouts of grumpiness had his servants considering alternative employment. To stave off a mass exodus, he raised their pay well beyond that of neighboring houses. As a result, Bertram's salary was nearly twice what other butlers received.

Max Higgins' father had nearly bankrupted the Greenley earldom with his drinking and gambling, but the Earl of Grump had managed to restore the earldom's accounts, pay off the debts, and provide his youngest sister, Beatrice, with a suitable dowry when she could finally marry.

That Lord Augustus, the second son of the fifth Duke of Huntington, had offered for her hand seemed too good to be true, but the two were apparently well suited. At last count, they had five children.

"A fire has been set in your bedchamber, sir,"

Bertram said before giving his master a slight bow. "Good night."

"Won't be anything good about it," Max grumbled, not bothering to glance in the direction of the butler. He snagged the next letter from the silver salver on his desk, his brows arching upon seeing the writing on the missive. He tore off the wax seal and unfolded the letter, relieved to see the slanted handwriting of his only son, Marcus.

Dear Father,

I hope my letter finds you in a better mood than the one I left you in upon my departure. I made it in time for classes Monday last and explained the reason for my absence to the dean. He may write to confirm my story—please do not reply with your usual vitriol as I would like to remain at Cambridge until I can complete my education.

I have made up what I missed during the week of my stay with you. Despite your insistence that I not be there, your illness had me quite vexed...

Max cursed as he threw his head back. "I wasn't ill," he said aloud. "And if I discover whoever it was that said I was..." He allowed the sentence to trail off, remembering that Bertram had already gone to bed. "Dammit."

He continued to read, his anger abating slowly.

I have conferred with several of my classmates regarding their plans for a Grand Tour. I know you were never able to take one given the wars with France, but I am hoping you'll allow me one. Despite his father's death (or maybe because of it), Grayson, or rather Billingsley now, I suppose, completed his term and has already left Cambridge for London. He will be off to Naples for his Grand Tour by week's end.

Blinking and then rereading the last sentence two more times, Max leaned forward in his chair.

Grayson, or rather Billingsley now implied the Marquess of Billingsley was dead.

Billingsley is dead?

The Marquess of Billingsley, dead?

Max glanced over at the stack of newspapers that had arrived over the past few months. Although he had intended to read *The Times* over his breakfasts in an attempt to keep up with news from London, he had lately opted to read the news-sheet from Birmingham. Reading about the events in the capital—especially when he wasn't there to see them for himself—seemed to put him in far fouler moods than usual.

As for David Grayson, Marquess of Billingsley, normally any mention of the man would have Max fuming in anger. Learning he was dead had Max flummoxed. Even in his worst moods, he didn't wish death for his fellow aristocrats. But his immediate reaction surprised him.

Good riddance, he thought darkly.

The Marquess of Billingsley had been the bane of his existence for two decades. He was part of the reason Max spent his days feeling irritable. Most of the reason he was not-so-affectionately known as the Earl of Grump.

Oh, he knew of the nickname his servants and neighbors used to refer to him. Knew it had been adopted by his fellow peers in the House of Lords. He had made it his goal in life to be in as poor a mood as possible. If he could not have the happiness they enjoyed in their marriages and with their families or in the hobbies they partook, then he didn't care if the stormy clouds that hovered over him darkened their lives, too.

He glanced back down at the letter, realizing his son had written more.

Do think on it and let me know, Father. Arrangements for travel must be made, and it's possible I might be able to join others who intend to go when the Lent term ends. A guide has already been arranged in Athens.

Aunt Beatrice wrote to me. Although she complains about her children (probably as much as you complained about me), she seems happy to have had them. Perhaps I'll meet my newest cousins before I depart for the Continent.

Please see to your health. I remain your devoted son, Marcus.

Max winced when he read the line *probably as much as you complained about me*. He had never intended for his son to hear his complaints. They hadn't been said because of anything Marcus did—well, except for the time he had let a frog loose in the parlor, or the time he had set a fire in his bedchamber, or the time Max had caught him racing the coach-and-four at midnight—but because of his generally grumpy mood. He couldn't help but wake up in a foul way every day.

Max tossed the letter back on his desk and was glad to see there were no others on the silver salver. Deciding to reply to his son right away, he pulled a sheet of stationery from one of the desk drawers and thought of how to respond.

Dear Marcus,

I apologize if you ever thought I complained about having fathered you. I was thrilled when you were born and am proud to call you my son. You'll make an excellent earl one day.

A knocking sound came from somewhere beyond his study, and he cursed. When it continued, the knocking growing louder and faster, he cursed again.
What the hell?

CHAPTER 3
AN UNFORTUNATE INCIDENT

arlier that evening, at a coaching inn near Bromsgrove, Worcester

"Do you think we can make it the rest of the way tonight?" Patience asked Jeffrey when a new matched pair of Cleveland bays had been changed out at The Golden Cross. Patience had been served tea and biscuits at the ancient coaching inn whilst they waited, and although she would have been fine with procuring a room at the next inn, she knew they had to be close to Grayson Park.

Jeffrey nodded. "I'll do my best, my lady," he said, obviously just as anxious to get to their destination. Although Patience had arranged regular rooms for him at the two coaching inns they had stayed in along the way, neither had offered much in the way of public rooms.

Bundled up against the cold in a caped greatcoat,

scarf and hat, Jeffrey looked twice his normal size. "Besides, I don't think there's another inn between here and Alveley that is open this time of the year, my lady."

Patience gave a start. "What?"

"It's winter, my lady. Not as many travelers, so not all the coaching inns are open."

Rolling her eyes, Patience realized why the stops along the way hadn't always been their usual haunts. "Of course. I'd quite forgotten," she murmured.

"I've been warned the road from here west is frozen, which means it may be a bit of a bumpy ride," he warned.

"Which means it's not muddy," Patience reasoned. She had been surprised to see that the new paint on the coach door still appeared black when they had pulled into a coaching yard their first night. From the condition of the roads outside of London, she had thought the door would end up covered in a layer of watery mud that might mix with the paint to form a permanent stain.

Jeffrey chuckled. "Yes, my lady, and the bridge over the Severn is open in Upper Areley."

The mention of Areley had Patience giving a start. "Oh, if we must," she murmured, knowing it really was the quickest way to get to Grayson Park. The route required they pass through lands belonging to the Greenley earldom, but at that time of the day, they would be unlikely to come across anyone.

Glad for the hot brazier at her feet—Jeffrey had

seen to some more coal at the last inn—Patience tried hard to keep her eyes open as the coach made its way into the lower tip of Staffordshire. In the dim twilight made more so by the gray clouds that filled the sky, she shivered at the reminder of who lived in this part of Staffordshire.

Twenty-two years ago, she'd had a completely different reaction to the thought of who lived here.

Twenty-two years ago, she fancied herself in love with the man. Even agreed to his proposal of marriage.

What would her life have been like if her father hadn't had other plans for her?

A happier marriage, to be sure, she considered, feeling guilt at the uncharitable thoughts she had of her father's edict. The least he could have done was warn her of his decision when she was younger. Explain how he couldn't afford a decent dowry. Tell her of his plans for her. Then she would have steered clear of forming any attachments. She wouldn't have accepted potential suitors. Wouldn't have allowed the brief courtship that had led to a most welcome marriage proposal.

A proposal she gladly accepted.

A proposal she never expected to have to end.

All because her father had arranged a betrothal on her behalf to the heir of the Billingsley marquessate.

Apparently when she was in leading strings!

Had she known betrothals were no longer allowed in England—at least from a legal perspective—she might have argued more vehemently with her father.

Stomped her slippered feet. Left his house in the middle of the night. Married the new Earl of Greenley, even if he didn't have two shillings to rub together.

Well, by then, Max Higgins had managed to improve the lot of the Greenley earldom. He probably had more than a few shillings in his pocket and some of his father's debt paid off.

Her father didn't think so, though.

Breaking off the engagement had been the hardest thing she had ever done. Harder even than giving birth to her son, for the pain she felt and the greater pain she had caused Maxwell Higgins had stayed with her for a very long time. That pain had then turned him into a most disagreeable sort. A grouchy earl intent on spreading his bad mood over whoever was within earshot.

And it was all her fault.

The memory of her last encounter with him swirled around in her thoughts as the carriage rumbled on through the frozen ruts in the road. She had nearly nodded off when a loud *crack* split the air and the coach came to a sudden halt.

Sure she heard the driver curse—Jeffrey Styles never cursed—Patience straightened in the squabs and dared a glance out the window. Despite the near full moon, darkness surrounded the coach. The jerk of the coach told her Jeffrey had stepped off the bench, and she heard his boot heels crunch on the frozen road.

Patience wasn't surprised when the coach door

opened. "What's happened?" she asked, before the driver poked his head in.

"A front wheel broke, my lady."

Resisting the urge to curse, Patience nodded. "Have you a sense of how far it is to Grayson Park?" she asked. Perhaps they were close. "Could we walk?"

Jeffrey seemed to think on it a moment before he shook his head. "Another four miles at least, maybe five," he replied, white clouds surrounding his face as he spoke. "And it's grown terribly cold." He disappeared a moment when the coach groaned and shifted. When he returned, he said, "We're not too far from the river, and there are lights still on at the end of a drive near here. Appears to be a large house."

Patience moved across the bench to take a look at where he indicated. "You say we're south of the river?" she asked, her brows furrowing.

"Yes, my lady."

"But we're still in Staffordshire?"

"Barely," he replied. "Crossed the border only a moment ago."

Sighing, Patience stared at the large manor house. Still lit from within, it sat at the end of the nearby drive. "Oh, all right," she murmured in resignation. "I'll go."

"Oh, I can go get help, my lady," Jeffrey argued. "You should stay in the coach."

She shook her head as she stepped out of the traveling coach, the sudden cold causing her breath to catch in her throat. "Trust me when I tell you it's far better that I go. I don't want your head bitten off."

Jeffrey blinked. "My lady?" he responded in confusion. He glanced up and down the road and then watched as the marchioness marched up the lane leading to the manor.

Closing the coach door, Jeffrey paused to ensure the horses were secure. "My lady," he called out. He pulled her valise from the coach and hurried to catch up to the marchioness. "Are you quite sure?"

Patience huffed. "Tell me, Mr. Styles. Have you ever heard of the Earl of Grump?" she asked as they crossed the semi-circular drive in front of a light gray sandstone manor. Crushed granite crunched beneath their boots as they made their way around a fountain featuring a marble mermaid surrounded by dolphins. Given the time of the year, no water emerged from the urn the mermaid held, and the round basin from which the dolphins appeared to jump was empty.

The driver slowed his steps. "The Earl of Greenley, you mean?" he countered, a worried expression forming on his face.

Patience nodded before she reached up and pounded the lion's head knocker several times. "The one and only," she replied on a long sigh.

CHAPTER 4
A PLEA FOR HOSPITALITY

*M*eanwhile, *in the Higgins House study*

Concentrating on the sound that continued from somewhere beyond the study, Max finally pushed away from his desk and made his way out to the hall. Barely lit from the gaslights at the top of the stairs, the caryatids and their marble busts lining the hall cast off long shadows onto the Turkish carpeting that led to the large front door.

The knocking was definitely coming from there.

Suspicious—who would come to Higgins House after dusk, especially at this time of the year?—Max made his way into the front salon. He had seen Bertram do the same in an attempt to determine the identity of a caller. Although its single window was closest to the entry, given its angle, Max couldn't make out whoever it was that was responsible for the incessant knocking. They were obviously standing very close to the door.

Whatever sized moon happened to be above the clouds made them appear as if they were a low gray ceiling. For as far as he could see, a layer of snow covered the ground. The thought of even more snow had Max frowning more than he already was.

The thought of an unwelcome guest had him near fuming.

Unless it's Marcus, he considered, immediately wondering why his son would have returned to Higgins House only a fortnight after leaving.

He quickly exited the salon and opened the front door, expecting to find Marcus on the other side of it.

The person who had been using the knocker was still hanging onto it, her gloved hand wound into the brass ring. She practically fell against the front of his body, a sound of startlement leaving her mouth open and her eyes wide as his arms instinctively wrapped around her to stop her forward movement.

For the briefest of moments, Max realized he hadn't held a woman's body in a very long time. From the familiar scent that tickled his nostrils, he was sure he had held her sometime in the past, perhaps during a dance. He next realized that he would enjoy kissing her strawberry-colored lips. He even considered doing so, the temptation to plunder the lush pillows causing him to dip his head a fraction. However, a young man wearing a black greatcoat and top hat was standing beyond the threshold with a look of horror on his face.

"Hello, Max," Patience murmured, finally able to

extract her hand from the knocker. She had to place it against his shoulder in an attempt to balance herself, her eyes rounding at the solidity of the earl's body.

Blinking, Max dared a glance at the young man again before his eyes darted once again to the woman. His brows furrowed as he drew his head back. "Patience?" he asked, his voice barely audible.

"*H*ow do, Max?" she asked as her gaze locked with his. When Max continued to mutely stare at her, she inhaled softly. "First, I wish to apologize profusely for having disturbed your evening. It was not my intention to do so," she said, once she had her feet firmly beneath her. She was still pressed against the earl, though, which had Jeffrey concerned.

"Do you require assistance, my lady?" the driver asked, about to step forward in an attempt to put himself between his mistress and Greenley.

"Who the hell are you?" Max asked, his sudden ire apparent.

The change in the man—from confusion to anger in only a moment— had Jeffrey cowering in fear. "Lady Billingsley's driver, my lord," he said as he quickly bowed. Although he had stepped into the hall, intending to shut the door, he retreated back onto the stoop.

"A wheel broke on the coach, right at the end of

your drive," Patience quickly said, fearing poor Styles was about to faint from fear.

Max turned his angry expression onto Patience. "Oh, so it's blocking the drive, I suppose," he groused.

Patience winced at hearing the words, as if he thought it had been done deliberately, but she was determined not to show fright in the earl's presence. "It's blocking the *road*. Not your drive," Patience clarified. "And seeing how it won't be possible to find a wheelwright this time of the night and we're still so far from Grayson Park, might we prevail upon your hospitality for the night? There are two horses and Mr. Styles, of course," she said in a rush. "And me."

Max's eyes rounded before they narrowed again. The word *hospitality* and him had probably never been associated with one another before. He swallowed, apparently aware his outburst had been an overreaction. "For how long?"

Hearing the suspicion in his voice, Patience straightened in an attempt to put some distance between their bodies. "Only for tonight," she replied. "I could probably walk the rest of the way to Grayson Park, but—"

"It's too damned cold," Max interrupted, apparently aware that the front door was still open when he could see white clouds from his breath in front of his face. He pulled Patience farther into the hall, and Jeffrey stepped into the house and closed the door behind him. He placed Patience's valise on the floor and began rubbing his gloved hands together in an attempt to warm them.

"Stable is around back," Max said with a jerk of his thumb. "You can stay in there with the horses—"

"Max," Patience whispered in a scolding voice.

"My groom and stable boy sleep in the loft above the stable," he countered, his mood growing dark again. "Doubt there's room for another up there."

Patience was about to respond, but Jeffrey beat her to it.

"It's all right, my lady. I don't mind," he said in a quiet voice. He was about to leave through the front door, but he gave her a look of worry. "But what about you?"

"Well, she's not going to sleep in the stable, if that's what you're thinking," Max yelled.

"Max," Patience whispered, followed by a scoff.

"Of course not, my lord," Jeffrey said before he bowed and slipped out through the door. It slammed behind him, a few flurries of snowflakes dancing about in his wake.

Patience turned to scold Max, but her words were caught in her throat when she saw how he gazed at her. For a moment, she thought him angry. For another, she thought him pensive. Mayhap a bit tongue-tied.

Was he about to kiss her?

The thought should have had her on her guard, but instead she experienced a brief memory of their last kiss. The one he had bestowed on her right before she had to give him the news that would end their fledgling betrothal.

She hadn't thought it possible to experience such pain in her chest and live through it. To cry so hard she couldn't catch her breath. Experience such guilt for which she wasn't responsible. But she'd had to on that day.

By the time Patience found her voice again, Max's brows were once again furrowed. "You keep doing that and they're going to stick like that," she warned, a finger moving to indicate his brow.

Max blinked. "What?"

"Your eyebrows," she replied. "When you pull them together like that, they make you look positively *fierce*," she claimed.

He deepened his scowl as he gazed at her. "Good," he responded. "Then they're working like they're supposed to."

For some reason, Patience found she couldn't keep a grin from lighting her face. It seemed Maxwell Higgins' reputation as the Earl of Grump was rather well earned. "Oh, Max," she whispered. "I am so very glad to see you again."

"Can't imagine why," he replied gruffly. "It's certainly not mutual."

Patience winced, unable to hide the hurt his words inflicted. "You have every right not to accommodate me," she said in a quiet voice. She dipped her head.

"After what I did to you. What I was forced to do all those years ago."

"Damned right," he countered, straightening to his nearly six foot height. When he noticed tears were collecting in the corners of her eyes, he scoffed. "Don't you dare cry," he warned.

His words only seemed to make matters worse, for Patience backed up and leaned against the front door, as if she needed the solid oak panel for support. The tears spilled over her lower lashes. "I hated him," she murmured as she fished for a hanky in her redingote pocket.

Max gave a start. "Him who?"

She rolled her eyes, which only sent more tears cascading down her cheeks. "Billingsley, the bastard," she replied. "And my father." Then she straightened, her gaze darting about the hall. "Where are your servants?" she asked suddenly. "Surely you have a butler?"

Max stared at her for what seemed like a very long time, as if he was trying to sort her words. Then he scoffed. "I sent him to bed," he replied. "The footman is off having a tumble with the barmaid at the Rooster's Crow, the cook and the scullery maid are no doubt abed, and the maids and laundress..." He paused and frowned. "They're around here somewhere, but I never see 'em."

"I can't imagine why," Patience murmured before she sniffled.

"I pay them well so I can be a grump," Max countered defensively. "Almost double what any of the landed gentry around these parts pay for servants."

"It's a wonder your earldom is solvent," Patience replied, an elegant eyebrow arching before she dabbed her nose with the white hanky.

Max appeared to fume for a moment. "Now see here. If you weren't a lady, I'd... I'd—"

"You would *what?*" she challenged. "Slap me? Challenge me to a duel?" Her fists went to her waist as she rose up on tiptoes in an effort to seem taller. "Throw me over your shoulder and take me up to your bedchamber? Have your way with me?"

She blinked when she heard her words spoken aloud.

She hadn't intended to challenge him in quite *that* way.

Hadn't intended to give him ideas he probably hadn't thought of himself.

Damnation!

She lowered her heels to the carpet and held her breath in anticipation of his response.

Max blinked, obviously left speechless. He stared at her for several seconds before he said, "I am a *gentleman*, my lady, and I shall escort you to a bedchamber. But you'll have to walk there of your own accord, because I have absolutely no intention of *carrying* you there."

It was Patience's turn to blink as she let out the breath she'd been holding. "All right," she agreed, aware her heart was pounding far faster than usual. She glanced behind her, glad to see Jeffrey had brought her valise into the house. Although it didn't have much in the way of clothes—she had thought they would make it to Grayson Park this night—it was comforting to have some of her own things with her. She bent and gripped the handles. "Lead the way," she said.

Max huffed and took the valise from her. "Allow me," he said. He turned toward the stairs, took three steps, and then paused to offer his arm.

Touched by the courtesy, Patience placed her arm on his and climbed the first flight of stairs with him in silence. "I cannot help but feel as if I've interrupted something," she said cautiously.

Pausing on the landing, Max gave a huff. "Stay here," he ordered.

Furrowing a brow, Patience watched as he quickly descended the stairs. Whatever light that might have come from below was suddenly extinguished, and Max was next to her a moment later. "What happened?" she asked in confusion.

"I left the damned gaslights on in the study," he replied, not bothering to apologize for his curse.

"So my arrival didn't interrupt something important?"

He shrugged. "I was writing a letter to Marcus."

Her eyes rounded. "He's at Cambridge, is he not?" she asked. "My son knows of him."

Remembering what Marcus had written in the

letter Max had read before her appearance, he scoffed. "The one you sent off on his Grand Tour?" he asked, a hint of disgust in his voice.

Patience inhaled softly. "How did you know?"

"Marcus wrote of it. Now *he* wants to go," he said, his voice sounding his complaint.

Unsure of why the idea of sending his son on a Grand Tour would have the earl annoyed, Patience regarded him warily. "Surely you'll send him when he's finished with his coursework," she guessed.

He gave her a quelling glance. "I haven't decided."

Patience displayed a curious expression. "I know *you* weren't able to go," she said, pity in her voice.

"How do you know that?" he asked gruffly as he led them down a wide corridor to a second set of stairs.

"As I recall, we were at war with France," she replied. "I rather doubt you would have wanted to go to the Kingdom of the Netherlands or... or Belgium for a European tour," she reasoned, her brow once again arching. Only soldiers and officers went to Europe back then. She rather doubted Max, the oldest son of an earl, would have served in the military. His younger brother might have, though. About to ask after him, she couldn't when Max huffed.

"Have you ever been to Europe?" he asked. "Paris, no doubt? For the latest in fashions for a marchioness?" he went on, his voice taking on a sing-song rhythm meant to sound condescending.

Patience scoffed. "Never," she said. "I'm not of a

mind to be unpatriotic when it comes to decorating my house. Or my wardrobe."

Max's eyes rounded, but he didn't put voice to a reply. Upon reaching the top of the second set of stairs, he waved her to a bedchamber. Opening the door, he was relieved to see that the master suite's fireplace was lit and the room was fairly warm. The dark blue counterpane had been folded back from the pillows, but the quilts and bed linens were still in place. "I'm afraid this is the only bedchamber available for the night," he said.

Patience inhaled softly, her gaze taking in the expanse of dark Turkish carpeting, ebony furnishings, and dark blue drapes. "It's beautiful," she breathed. "A bit on the masculine side, but—"

"That's because this is *my* bedchamber," he interrupted, dropping her valise into a nearby chair.

Stepping backward toward the door, Patience regarded him with a look of shock. "Oh. Well, there must be another bedchamber I can use for the night."

"There is not. It's winter, and I'm too Scotch to have the fireplaces lit for the other rooms to be kept warm," he explained.

"Oh. All right. I'm sure I'll be fine in one of these chairs," she offered, not about to suggest he be the one to sleep in a chair. The very last thing she wanted to do was anger him even more than he already was.

"You'll sleep in the bed," he stated.

Patience visibly relaxed. "That's rather generous of you, Max."

"I don't see how," he replied. "I'll be in the bed as well. It'll be good to have another body to help warm it."

For the first time that night, Max's expression wasn't dark or moody or murderous. He actually appeared rather friendly, and it was everything Patience could do to keep a pleasant expression on her own face.

This was going to be a long night.

CHAPTER 5
GROOMS CONFIDE

eanwhile, outside the Higgins House stable

Winding his scarf tighter around his neck, Jeffrey Styles hurried back to the traveling coach to unhitch the horses. Despite wearing several pairs of socks under his boots, he could barely feel his toes due to the cold. For the brief moment he had been inside Higgins House, he had relished the warmth even while fearful for his mistress.

His gloved hands fumbled with the leather straps as he considered what she might be experiencing at the hands of the Earl of Greenley. From her reaction to the man and from the way the grouch had stared at her, Jeffrey knew they had met at some point in the past. They'd probably been friends. After all, what marchioness called an earl by his Christian name? What earl called a marchioness by her Christian name?

Jeffrey didn't dare consider the possibility that they might have at one time been lovers. For the entire time he had worked for the Billingsley marquessate, Patience Grayson had been a most proper aristocratic lady. As far as he knew, she had never hosted a lover nor met one surreptitiously instead of attending a London entertainment.

He would know.

He had been her driver for nearly a decade.

On the other hand, Billingsley had been a scoundrel, squiring his string of mistresses about London with no regard for his marriage vows. Jeffrey had been secretly glad when the marquess died. Glad for the marchioness, glad for his son, and glad for the servants who worked in the Grayson townhouse in Westminster.

Gathering the leather reins into one hand, he gently tugged until the horses complied and were clear of the coach. Capturing the handle of one of the coach lanterns in his other hand, he trudged the short snow-covered drive to Higgins House. Snowflakes fell around him, but they danced away as he and the Cleveland bays made their way toward the stable.

Both horses seemed to understand they were headed for warmth and food, for they neighed and nickered despite his attempts to keep them quiet.

Startled by the sudden appearance of an older man carrying a pitchfork, Jeffrey let out a yelp.

"Who goes there?" The baritone voice held a hint of

menace, and the pitchfork lifted so its tines were pointed in Jeffrey's direction.

One of the horses neighed loudly as his head bobbed up and down, as if he thought the query directed to him. "Styles, sir," Jeffrey replied. "I'm the driver for the Marchioness of Billingsley. We was headed to Grayson Park."

The pitchfork lowered as the other man peered beyond where Jeffrey stood. "Coach broke down?" he guessed.

Jeffrey nodded. "Wheel broke, sir. His lordship said I could put the horses in the stable and spend the night in there with 'em."

The older man scoffed. "Well, the horses are welcome to stay in there, but I'll not have you sleeping with them. Come on," he said as he took the reins of one of the horses and led them to a gray stone building behind the manor house. "Name's Cruthers," the groom offered. Given Jeffrey carried a lantern, he didn't offer his hand. "The stableboy is Hastings. He's asleep upstairs. Damn kid can sleep through a thunderstorm."

"I appreciate the hospitality," Jeffrey said, marveling at the size of the stable before him. Even if it housed equipage in addition to horses, he thought it large enough to accommodate a dozen of the beasts. "His lordship must race horses, I'm guessing?"

Cruthers scoffed again as he grinned. "Did a long time ago, but he's only got two walkers now. Goes for a long ride on part of his earldom every day. Switches out which horse he rides so they both get regular exercise," he explained. He paused to allow Jeffrey to open a large door. The earthy scents of hay and manure wafted past their noses as they led the Cleveland bays into the building. "He might be a grouch with humans, but his lordship is good with the beasties."

Jeffrey boggled at seeing the condition of the stable's interior. He was sure it was cleaner than some tenant farmers' cottages. An old black traveling coach was parked at one end where there was another set of doors, and eight stalls—four on opposite walls—looked as if they were new. Large black hinges secured the stall doors to their posts, and each door had a black latch. Two of the stalls were occupied by a pair of gray Irish walkers who showed a good deal of interest in the Cleveland Bays. A series of nickers and neighs had Cruthers chuckling.

"Should I be worried about her ladyship?" Jeffrey asked as he moved a wheelbarrow filled with straw to one of the empty stalls. Cruthers used the pitchfork to spread the straw bedding. "His lordship didn't exactly greet her very kindly," he added.

Chuckling again, Cruthers led one of the bays into a stall. "She'll be fine. The earl's bark is worse than his bite. And he could use the company. Reminds him to be civil."

Jeffrey opened the other stall door and led the second bay into it as the groom filled the wheelbarrow with hay from a nearby stack. "I think her ladyship knows him. She called him Max," Jeffrey said, remembering how odd it had been to hear the two use their Christian names. Rather than pushing herself away from Lord Greenley when she had been pulled into the house, her hand still caught in the lion's head knocker, she had remained in his arms. Hadn't made a peep of protest.

She had the courage to scold him, though. Several times.

Although Lord Greenley seemed determined to be a grouch, there had been a few moments where her quiet rebukes had him capitulating. Had his harsh features softening. Had his raised voice lowering.

As if she could tame him.

Perhaps she could. The grump could certainly use a lesson in manners.

Jeffrey glanced over at the groom to discover his brows furrowed in thought. "What is it?"

"Marchioness of Billingsley, did you say?" Cruthers asked.

"Indeed."

Huffing, Cruthers gave a shrug. "Wouldn't be surprised, with Grayson Park being so close and all," he said. "Or..." A thoughtful expression crossed his face before he displayed a wide grin.

"Or what?" Jeffrey countered, curious as to what the groom found so amusing.

Cruthers gave a one-shouldered shrug. "She could be the one."

His brows furrowing, Jeffrey stared at the groom. "The one?" he repeated.

A chuckle once again erupted from the groom. "There's talk our Lord Greenley was once thrown over by a woman. Although he took solace in the arms of another—his wife, God rest her soul—he apparently never got over his first love," he explained as he patted his chest with one gloved hand.

"He was *married?*" Jeffrey asked in alarm. He immediately took pity on whoever it was who had dared to marry the grump.

"He was. Sweet woman, her ladyship she was, but she died a couple of days after she gave him his heir. Marcus is his son's name," he explained. "Some say she died because his lordship was such a grouch, but I don't believe that."

Jeffrey nodded his understanding and then hauled pails of water into each stall. Before long, he could feel his feet tingling as they warmed. "Well, hopefully we won't need your hospitality beyond this evening," he murmured. "Is there a wheelwright nearby?"

Cruthers saw to refilling the pails of water for the two walkers. "There's one over in Kidderminster. We can send you there with the footman in the morning," Cruthers offered. "Fields has to go anyway to pick up my wife's order. She's the cook, by the way," he added as he nodded in the direction of the house.

"That would be most appreciated," Jeffrey commented, his gaze following the groom's. "Tell me, is his lordship as grouchy with his household staff as he was with me?"

Cruthers chuckled. "He can be, but he pays nearly twice what any of the other gentry pay for servants in these parts, and most know how to avoid crossing his path in the house, so it's worth an occasional dressing down." His eyes suddenly widened. "You might even know one of 'em," he added, his hands crossing his chest so he could warm them.

"Oh?" Jeffrey couldn't remember meeting any Higgins House staff in the past. "How's that?"

"Bertram—he's the butler—he hired one of the housemaids from Grayson Park about a month ago. Needed a replacement for one who'd quit 'cuz his lordship made her so nervous she practically fainted every single day."

Staring at the groom for several seconds, Jeffrey swallowed.

Cruthers noticed. "You look like you seen a ghost," he commented.

Shaking his head, Jeffrey asked, "Would you know the maid's name, by chance?"

"Well, of course. We eat our meals with the household staff," he claimed. "Ludlow is her name. Right pretty girl, but she mostly keeps to herself."

Jeffrey exhaled. "That she does," he murmured, a mix of sadness and confusion crossing his features.

"So... you *do* know her," Cruthers countered.

Nodding, Jeffrey slipped a hand into his greatcoat

and felt for the lump in his waistcoat pocket. The gold ring had cost him a half-year's wages, but he knew it was worth it. "I do. I've been planning to make her my wife these past five years or so. Just needed to save up some more blunt is all," he explained.

Cruthers drew back as if he'd been slapped. "Well, I hope you're not expecting her to give up her position. She probably makes more 'an you do," he teased.

Wincing, Jeffrey realized his plans might require a slight modification. "How far is it to Grayson Park from here?"

Cruthers seemed to think on it a moment before he announced, "Four miles, according to his lordship." He quickly added, "Now I'm not saying a marriage would be impossible, but you might only be able to see one another on her day off."

Jeffrey nodded his understanding. He had already come to the same conclusion. "It's better than how often we see one another now," he reasoned. For a moment, he contemplated going to the servants' entrance of the main house and asking the butler if Janet might still be awake. The thought that the grouchy Earl of Greenley might open the back door like he had opened the front door earlier that evening had him changing his mind.

"You can see Ludlow in the morning. At breakfast," Cruthers said as he waved to a set of narrow stairs that led up to the loft. "Let's get you upstairs. There's a bunk with an extra bed, but you'll have to take the bottom. Hastings sleeps up top."

"I don't mind," Jeffrey said as he used the lantern to light their way. He followed the groom up the stairs, basking in the much warmer air in the loft.

Not bothering to undress, he settled onto the bunk and listened intently, afraid at any moment he would hear the Marchioness of Billingsley screaming for help.

But it was Janet Ludlow on whom his thoughts came to rest when only the sounds of the horses below could be heard. He imagined how her lips would feel against his as he kissed her good night, and then he finally fell asleep.

CHAPTER 6
DEALING WITH A BEAST

eanwhile, in the master bedchamber of Higgins House

Despite having agreed to the arrangements they had discussed upon arriving in the bedchamber, Patience was having second thoughts about sharing Max's bed. "Are you quite sure there isn't another bedchamber I might be able to use this night?" she asked when she emerged from the dressing room.

Wearing only her chemise beneath a humongous robe, she felt terribly self-conscious. The man's garment was so large, the front edges could probably wrap around her body and to her back, and there would be still be room for another person inside.

She gave a start when her gaze locked onto Max.

Given his dressing gown was wrapped around her body meant it wasn't wrapped about him. In fact, he wasn't wearing anything. He had been doffing his pantaloons when she hurried into the dressing chamber and now had just pulled his shirt from his body. "You're naked," she said in alarm, her eyes rounding in surprise.

Max straightened and gave her a quelling glance. "Yes. That's what happens when I'm not wearing any clothes," he remarked dryly.

Rather than turn her head—Patience found she couldn't even if she had wanted to—she froze. Her gaze swept over his body, stunned to see it was nothing like what she had imagined a real man's body to look like.

Not that she had given it much thought in the past.

Patience couldn't recall ever even wondering what was beneath his shirt, waistcoat, and pantaloons. Now that he was on full display, she found she was more curious than embarrassed. From how he had felt beneath her hands earlier that evening, she knew his body was firm. His chest and shoulders hard. It seemed as if there was nothing soft about the man.

There was a dusting of dark hair covering most of his chest, but then it narrowed into an arrow lower on his torso. "What are those?" she asked, pointing to his abdomen.

Max furrowed his brows, as if he hoped to appear as fierce as possible. "What are *what?*" he repeated, annoyed she hadn't turned around. The least she could have done was allow him to climb under the covers. Despite the fire, the room wasn't particularly warm now that he was undressed.

Patience moved closer, her hand stretching out to

indicate the area under his chest. He sucked in a breath, and his abdominal muscles clearly defined the six areas she indicated. She gasped and pulled her hand away.

"That would be my belly," he stated.

Patience gave him a quelling glance. "But it's not soft and... and round," she said in awe.

His annoyance barely abated. "Like Billingsley's?" he countered. "You prefer soft and round?"

Opening her mouth to respond, Patience reached out and placed her palm on his skin. Her fingertips trailed along the indentations as she stared in wonder. "I had never given it any consideration," she whispered.

Not having experienced a woman's touch in a very long time, Max inhaled sharply and knew he could no longer control what was about to happen. Knew he could no longer think of something other than what was under his dressing gown. Could no longer keep his desire from showing.

Well, it served her right.

After what she had done all those years ago, he wasn't about to apologize for what was happening directly south of where she was practically tickling him. The cool air wasn't keeping his cock in check any longer.

• • •

"Oh, my God," Patience said, nearly breathless.

Max jerked his head to regard her, a grin replacing his frown. "I don't think anyone's ever likened it to a deity before," he said as he chuckled.

Patience scoffed as she gave him a scolding glance. Despite her attempt to turn away, she could not. "It's so straight and... thick and..." She reached down and tapped her finger on the end of it, quickly pulling it away when the member bobbed slightly. "Alive!"

His grin widening at hearing her words, Max moved to the bed. He grasped several layers of linens and blankets in his fist and flipped them halfway down the bed. "I take it Billingsley's didn't compare?" he asked, about to situate himself under the cool covers. A thought that his cock wouldn't take kindly to the cold had him pausing.

Inhaling softly, Patience seemed about to respond and then sniffed. "I'm sure I wouldn't know."

Max blinked. Had he heard her correctly? "How could you *not* know?"

Patience's eyes widened as a look of uncertainty crossed her face. "What do... what do you mean?"

It was Max's turn to scoff. "You have a son," he said with more force than he intended. "You must have seen Billingsley's prick a time or two."

Shoving her hands into the pockets of the dressing robe, Patience was barely aware that it had opened in the front to reveal that she wore only her chemise beneath. With her trunk still on the back of the traveling coach, she had only her valise with her, and she hadn't packed it expecting to have to spend another night on the road before their arrival at Grayson Park. "I'm quite sure I would have remembered seeing it if I had seen it," she said with a huff. "It was always dark. Billingsley preferred making love in the dark."

Max regarded her with a furrowed brow for a moment. "Then he was a fool," he said, stepping away from the bed.

Her chin rising slightly, Patience asked, "Why do you say that?" When she saw how he approached her in all his glory, his cock leading the way, she swallowed. She likened it to a wooden pike, given its girth and the way the pointy end seemed about to poke her.

"Because he wouldn't have been able to see you," he whispered. "In all your glory."

Patience inhaled sharply, suddenly aware of how close he stood. Of how he smelled of musk and citrus. Of how his eyes darkened.

She had always liked that about him.

She knew when he was about to kiss her. When he was about to pull her into his arms and ravage her lips with his lips as one of his large hands encased a breast and pressed and molded it. Even now, all these years later, she sensed he was about to kiss her. "Well, I was... I was wearing a night rail, of course," she murmured, realizing she hadn't responded to his claim.

"But you aren't tonight," he replied, grasping the

edges of the dressing robe to pull it more open than it already was. His sudden move had her arms trapped in the sleeves of the robe, her hands still in the pockets.

She gasped as the warmth of the heavy fabric disappeared. Cool air had her nipples coming to attention. The thin chemise, nearly translucent, did nothing to hide them, nor the dark hair at the apex of her thighs. "It's in my trunk," she whispered, stunned she could carry on the conversation, what with heat pooling at the top of her thighs and flutterbies having an orgy in her abdomen.

This time it wasn't his hand that covered her breast—both of his still clutched the edges of the dressing robe—but rather his mouth. For all at once, it descended on one of the fabric-covered globes, his tongue laving over the protruding nipple before his lips captured it and he suckled.

Patience inhaled sharply, stunned at the sensations his ministrations created. Stunned by how his cock pressed into her belly, the fabric of the chemise barely separating their bodies. Her knees felt weak, and she was about to cry out when his mouth moved up and his lips left a trail of kisses above the neckline of the chemise.

Perhaps he sensed she was about to collapse, or perhaps he merely wished to get her onto the bed, but only a moment before she would have crumpled to the floor, he had her in his arms and onto the bed.

If the linens were cold, she didn't notice. If

anything was cold, she didn't notice. Her entire body felt as if it had turned molten on the inside. Billingsley had never had her feeling like this. Never had her so weak-kneed and in need of him. Never so discombobulated. Never so unable to speak.

"Did you ever *beg* for him?" The words ground out of Max, his hot breath warming her neck and shoulder. His entire body seemed to cover hers, but she didn't feel the weight of him.

"No, of course not," she whispered.

Max stilled his movements, his brow furrowing as he pulled his face away from her neck. "Would you have begged for me?"

Patience blinked several times, moaning when he lifted his body and hovered over her, his straight arms holding him up. A quick look down had her realizing his cock was straight, too, and poised to penetrate her if she merely spread her legs. "As I recall, I did beg for you," she replied in a hoarse whisper.

Staring down at her, Max held still and took several labored breaths. "Why don't I remember that?"

Patience managed to lift one shoulder in the pillow, as if to shrug. "You weren't there."

Her simple words had Max rolling over and sitting up on the bed. He quickly covered his lower half with the bed linens, and when she saw what he'd done, she scrambled to get under the covers as well. When she was done, they were sitting side-by-side, a pile of pillows at their backs.

Max glanced over at her. "Who were you talking to when you begged for me?" he asked. He ran a hand through his dark hair, his fingers leaving it spiky in a few places.

Reaching over to smooth his hair back into place, Patience said, "My father, of course. Right after he informed me I would be marrying Billingsley."

Max gave a start. "Your father?" he repeated.

"Well, it certainly wasn't *my* idea to marry David Grayson," she argued, dipping her head when she realized she had raised her voice. "He was old enough to be my father, and I'd already set my cap on you, and I thought you'd had the forethought to ask his permission—"

"I was on my way to doing so when you threw me over," he interrupted, his anger once again apparent.

"I didn't *throw you over*," she countered, sitting up straighter. "I couldn't lift you if I'd wanted to," she added, her chin thrust into the air.

He gave her a quelling glance. "You know exactly what I meant," he said in a voice filled with warning.

She seemed about to say something else before she took a steadying breath. "Father had already made arrangements for my betrothal, but he didn't see fit to inform me," she explained, her voice rising in indignation. "Otherwise, I would have gladly wed you, although now I cannot for the life of me imagine what had me so attracted to you."

His eyes narrowed. "As I recall, you enjoyed our kisses."

About to respond, Patience took a steadying breath. She seemed to think on his comment a moment before she nodded. "I did," she agreed.

"You also liked it when I cupped your lovely breasts with my hands," he accused, itching to do it right then and there.

She nodded. "Oh, yes. And what you were doing a few moments ago with your mouth was quite thrilling."

Her unexpected compliment calmed him somewhat. "Thank you," he replied. He glanced over at her. "I don't think you ever touched my belly like you did earlier," he commented. "It was quite... erotic."

Her eyes swept over his uncovered torso and snapped back up to meet his. "That's because I never saw you naked before," she reasoned. "And exactly what muscles are those that make those six pooches on your belly?" she asked as she waved a finger in their general direction.

Despite his attempt to remain angry—or at least annoyed—Max chuckled. "I told you. They're... they're abdominal muscles," he stammered.

She grimaced. "Well, how did you get them? You look like one of those Greek statues in the British Museum," she murmured before she paused a moment. "Well, except for the size of your..." She pointed to his blanket-covered lap. "Prick," she finished. "I'm quite sure I haven't seen a Greek statue with one quite like yours."

Max's eyes rounded. "What the hell were you doing looking at naked Greek statues?" he asked, not bothering to apologize for cursing.

"Research, of course," she replied. At his look of disbelief, she added, "With my son, Thomas. I was making sure he was prepared for his Grand Tour."

At the mention of Thomas, Max glanced down to where his feet tented the bed linens. "It's hard to believe he's already old enough," he murmured in a whisper.

Patience wondered at the change in his mood. "Only a year older than your son," she countered quietly. "I was very sorry to hear what happened to your countess."

He shrugged. "I think she died on purpose," he groused.

"Maxwell Higgins, you brute!" Patience scolded. "How can you say such a thing?"

"Because I was a beast," he replied on a sigh. "I am a beast."

Leaning away from him lest he prove his words, Patience tried to imagine him worse than she had seen him earlier that evening. "You are rather grumpy," she acknowledged. "But I know you're not a beast," she continued as she placed a hand on his arm. About to say more, she couldn't when he huffed.

"What do you know? You haven't been around me in over two decades," he accused as he shook off her hold. He crossed his arms over his chest, which had his upper arms bulging.

Patience angled her head to one side and regarded him with an expression of sadness. "I wanted to be," she whispered, angling her body toward him. She lifted a finger to trace the muscles in his arm.

All the air and indignation seemed to go out of Max all at once. "So why has it taken you so long to pay a call?" he asked, his voice cracking slightly. He didn't try to push away her questing finger, but his gaze followed it for a moment as if he was suspicious of where it might end up.

"I've only been a widow a few months," Patience replied. "I'm supposed to be in mourning, so I thought to spend it at the house in Shropshire. Maybe see to the gardening. Do some drawing. Maybe do a painting or two."

"*Then* were you going to pay a call?" he challenged.

She lifted her chin. "I was rather hoping *you* would pay a call on me," she countered. "I was planning to send a note inviting you for tea."

He grimaced. "I didn't know that Billingsley had died until Marcus mentioned it in his last letter," he said on a huff.

Patience blinked. "What? How could you not—?"

"I only receive news from London by way of *The Times,*" he interrupted. "And from the occasional correspondence my man of business sends me."

"It was in the *Times*," she argued. "Quite an impressive article, in fact."

He sighed. "I will admit I haven't been reading the

London newspapers," he said in his own defense. He turned his gaze on her. "I don't suppose Billingsley perished in your bed?"

"Maxwell Marcus Michael Matthew Higgins, you *brute!*"

Max blinked before a huge grin split his face. "You remembered all my names," he said in wonder.

Patience took one of the pillows from behind her and swung it at him. "Of course I remember all your names," she replied just as the pillow landed against his chest. "How else would I be able to scold you so I know you'll understand how incensed you've made me?"

Try as he might, Max couldn't hide his amusement. "I don't recall you ever scolding me before," he commented.

"That's because I didn't have to," she countered, annoyed the pillow had done nothing to make him sorry for what he'd said.

Max sobered as he stared at her. "How *did* he die?"

Patience recoiled before she once again lifted her chin. "Besides bitter and angry?"

Recoiling from the vehemence in her voice, Max lifted a hand as if to ward off a blow. "What the hell happened?"

All at once and for the first time since she had come to his bedchamber, Patience looked as if she would take her leave. Tears pricked the corners of her eyes, and she sniffled. "He thought *I* was having an *affaire*. With the footman," she spat out.

Max frowned. "Were you?" For some reason, he couldn't imagine Patience Seward Grayson having an *affaire* with anyone. Him included.

"Of course not," she replied, once again indignant. "Billingsley was going mad, I tell you. He imagined the most unlikely scenarios. He accused Thomas of being a bastard. Said I'd tricked him into marrying him, and that I'd bedded every earl in Britain just to get back at him because he had once complained about an invoice from a modiste."

"That's a lot of earls," Max commented.

"Almost two-hundred," she countered as she nodded.

"For how much was the invoice?"

Patience scoffed and rolled her eyes. "I don't remember," she whined. "But I think it was for a ball-gown, so probably more than usual."

Displaying a rather sad expression, Max said, "I never had the opportunity to buy you a ballgown."

Patience gave a start. "I should hope not," she replied. "If anyone thinks you're grumpy now, just think of how much worse you'd be if *you* were receiving invoices from a modiste."

A look of hurt crossed his face. "I didn't mind when Madeline had clothes made," he countered. "I never complained. Not once."

Patience swallowed at hearing his claim. At hearing how quiet he'd become. At seeing how calm he was. She was surprised at the streak of jealousy she felt at hearing his mention of his wife, though. "So you... you liked her?" she asked in a whisper. "Madeline?"

He nodded. "I did. I think I even loved her. In my own way," he grudgingly replied. "Of course, you never realize how much you want someone until they're not around anymore."

She dipped her head. "I don't miss Billingsley one bit," Patience said in a whisper. "I don't think Thomas does, either." Wincing, she asked, "Does that make me an awful person?"

Max shook his head. "Do you think he ever loved you?"

Patience looked as if she might cry again, but instead she swallowed. "No. He once told me he respected me. Said I was a good marchioness. That I did all the right things and didn't embarrass him, so there's that," she reasoned. "I think he loved one of his mistresses, though. Maybe more than one of them."

Sitting up straighter, Max regarded her with disbelief. "He had *you* for a wife, and he kept *mistresses*?" he asked in a loud voice.

"Well, now all of Staffordshire knows," Patience said as she rolled her eyes.

"He was a damned fool!" Max went on, ignoring her remark. "If I'd known, why... why I'd—"

"You'd what?" she countered, daring him to finish his thought.

"I would have challenged him to a duel in

Wimbledon Common," he claimed. "Then I would have shot his balls off. He would have bled out right then and there. Problem solved."

Patience leaned away from him, shocked by the violence in his words. That he would have done it for her had her reaching for his hand. "Thank you," she murmured. "My champion." She glanced down to see the bed linens had tented where his body was bent. "Why did you allow me to see your... to see your prick like you did?"

A tinge of red seemed to creep up Max's neck and face. "I wouldn't say I allowed it as much as I couldn't avoid it," he groused. "You're wearing my dressing robe," he reminded her.

"You could have turned around," she reasoned.

"Then you would have seen my bare arse," he replied.

She couldn't suppress her smirk. "Does *it* look like it belongs to a Greek god?"

Max gave his response a moment of thought before he said, "I ride my horse every day, so it's not exactly soft and round if that's what you're asking." His eyes darkened as he watched her reaction. Watched how her face colored with a pink blush. Heard her inhalations of breath.

"Oh," she finally replied, managing to make the word two-syllables.

The breathy response had Max's cock hardening even more. "I guess I wanted you to see it," he admitted. "Thought to show it off, since I'm quite sure it's larger than Billingsley's ever was."

Scoffing, Patience squeezed his hand. "Although I never actually saw his, I can assure you that yours is... larger," she murmured.

Max interlaced his fingers with hers. "It's all your fault, you know."

Patience blinked and straightened against the pillows. "*I* didn't remove your pantaloons," she argued.

He gave her a quelling glance. "I couldn't exactly leave them on." They sat in silence a moment as his thumb rubbed over the back of her hand. Dipping his head, he asked, "Did it frighten you?"

Her gaze having dropped to their hands, Patience felt her embarrassment increase. "I wouldn't say *fright* was the first impression I had," she replied, one of her brows arching.

"Oh?"

She glanced up to meet his gaze. "I think it was more about seeing you looking like some sort of Greek god. As if you were demanding to be worshipped."

"Ah," he murmured, a grin tugging at the edge of his lips. All of a sudden, he looked years younger. "Do you suppose you could be one of my subjects?" he asked, his voice sounding as if he might be teasing her. He slowly sobered. "Or maybe my goddess?"

Patience swallowed and regarded him with a look of uncertainty. "I suppose it depends if you're a vengeful god or if you're a benevolent god," she replied.

Max heard the quaver in her voice. He wondered if she was frightened of him and decided then and there he didn't want her frightened. He wanted her to like him. Wanted her to feel for him what he had felt for her all those years ago. From what she had said earlier, about how she had been forced to end their betrothal, he thought perhaps she really had loved him. "I could be benevolent," he claimed.

Her gaze settled on his lips and then on his bare chest. "Benevolent enough to allow one of your worshippers to stay in your temple?"

He glanced down at her hand as his thumb brushed over the back of hers. "Will you stay?" he asked, lifting her hand to kiss her knuckles.

Thinking it would take at least a day to find someone to fix the coach wheel, Patience realized she might require his hospitality for more than this night and the next. "May I?"

He nodded.

"Will you be grumpy?"

He half-shrugged. "Probably," he admitted.

She grinned and then giggled. "Whatever can I do to help tame the beast?"

He glanced over at her and then around the room. "Are you feeling chilly?"

She shook her head. "I'm actually quite comfortable."

"Enough to take off my dressing gown?"

Patience didn't bother replying, instead shrugging her arms out of the garment. "What now?"

Max realized if he didn't accept her offer right then and there, he might never get another chance. "I have an idea," he replied.

CHAPTER 7
HOUSEMAIDS SPY ON A
VISITOR

Earlier, on the servants' floor of Higgins House

Dressed in her white night rail and a pair of woolen socks, and wrapped in a thick robe, Janet Ludlow covered herself with the bed linens against the chill of her small room and settled her head into the pillow. She opened the gothic novel she had pulled from the library shelves on the first floor of Higgins House earlier that day and aimed it so the flame from the candle lamp could illuminate the pages.

Not a novel she would expect an earl to have in his collection. In fact, she wouldn't have guessed the earl to have any works of fiction, so she reasoned the half-dozen shelves containing novels had been filled by someone else.

Probably by a woman. Or several of them. Janet knew he'd had a wife at one time—the mother of his son, Marcus. He had no doubt had a mother of his own that would have stayed at Higgins House on occasion. Two sisters as well, if she could believe what Fields had told her the first week of her employment. Given the age of the house, it was likely there had been several generations of Higgins women before that.

Whoever had seen to stocking the library, she silently thanked them. Janet had made it a habit of reading before going to sleep almost every night since she had learned how to read.

At Grayson Park, she had been given permission by Lady Billingsley to help herself to any book in the library. At Higgins House, she had been led to believe the Earl of Greenley would probably turn down her request simply because he was a grouch.

So she borrowed books without asking.

One thing she had learned since taking the position at the manor house was that the earl rarely visited any of the rooms on the first floor. His bedchamber was on the second floor, and the dining room and his study were on the ground floor. Other than those three rooms and the stable, he didn't seem to go anywhere else in the house.

As a result, the first floor parlor and library seemed safe refuges in which to hide.

Before Janet finished reading the first page of the book, the sound of neighing horses had her listening intently. The earl's horses were never outside this time of the night, and they couldn't be heard when they were in the stone stable.

Had they escaped?

A soft knock at the door had her giving a start. "Who's there?" she called out.

"Ludlow, it's me, Agnes."

Janet set aside the book and threw off the covers, wincing when she realized all the warmth she had generated would be lost before she could return to bed. She hurried to the door and opened it. "What is it?"

Agnes Sherman didn't reply but quickly moved to the window. She pulled aside the cotton curtain and waved for Janet to join her. "Someone's here," she whispered. "Did you hear if we was expectin' anyone?"

With her window facing the front of the house, Janet would normally be able to see anyone coming down the drive and parking in the semi-circular area near the entrance to Higgins House. That is, if she was in her quarters during the daylight hours. Since she wasn't, this was first time she could recall seeing anyone approach the manor house.

In this instance, it was a man leading two large horses. Rather noisy horses given their neighing and nickering could be heard all the way to her window.

"I didn't hear," Janet replied. She cupped her hands around her face to block out the candlelight. "Seems odd he would leave his coach way out there," she added, spotting the black equipage near the end of the drive. At this time of the night, she normally wouldn't have been able to see to the road, but the layer of snow-laden clouds seemed to be illuminated from above—

probably by the moon—and the fresh layer of snow on the ground cast the property in varying shades of gray.

Agnes' attention was still on the man below. "He stopped," she murmured. "Oh, dear," she quickly added.

Janet stood on tiptoe and angled her head to get a better vantage. "Well, he's definitely not expected," she murmured when she could finally make out Mr. Cruthers threatening the visitor with a pitchfork.

"Must be who was knocking so hard at the front door," Agnes whispered.

"Knocking?" Janet repeated.

"Heard it in my room," Agnes claimed. "Or rather felt it, I suppose. Went on for some time 'afore his lordship opened the door."

Frowning, Janet stepped back from the window. The cold emanating from the glass had her shivering. She could only imagine how much colder it was on the other side. "How do you know it wasn't Bertram who opened the door?"

"He's abed," Agnes replied, her gaze still on the men below. "Heard him come up awhile ago. Come on," she urged as she rushed out of the room.

Janet scoffed but followed the other housemaid out to the thin corridor and around the corner. "Where are we going?" she whispered.

"Empty room that looks down on the stable," Agnes replied.

Rolling her eyes, Janet joined Agnes in a larger

room featuring two beds and a small dresser. The room's only window was located between the beds, and they moved to it and watched as the visitor and Mr. Cruthers made their way to the stable. "He may not be expected, but Cruthers is lettin' him in."

"I suppose he's the driver for the coach that's parked at the end of the drive," Janet said in a whisper.

"Which means he's probably spendin' the night," Agnes said with some excitement.

"Which means we'll meet him at breakfast in the morning," Janet reasoned. "Now can we go to bed?"

"He's not old," Agnes murmured, finally able to see the driver when the light from the lantern he carried illuminated his face as he moved to open the stable door. "Can't tell for sure, but I think he's right handsome," she added with a grin. "Decent coat and hat. Good boots."

Janet scoffed. "You cannot tell all that from this distance," she said in a hushed voice, even as she was coming to the same conclusion.

When the driver turned to lead one of the horses into the stable, his gaze lifted, and for a quick moment, he appeared to be staring at them. Agnes inhaled sharply and stepped back, but Janet merely blinked.

A curious expression on her face, she finally retreated from the window when the stable doors closed.

"What is it?" Agnes asked when she caught Janet's look of surprise.

"He looked familiar, is all," Janet whispered, not adding that she was fairly sure she knew who it was.

"A driver and two horses and a coach," Agnes murmured.

Janet nodded. "Which means his lordship has a caller. One who is spending the night," she reasoned. She couldn't imagine the Earl of Greenley offering hospitality to anyone, or anyone who would want his hospitality. But then, if the driver was who she thought he was, then she was fairly sure she knew who had been knocking at the front door.

A hand went to her middle as her shoulders slumped. *Poor woman.*

Excitement had Agnes nearly bouncing on the balls of her stockinged feet, though. "Well, it can't be his son," she said, as she thought the visitor might be someone important. "Mr. Cruthers wouldn't threaten his driver with a pitchfork."

"It's someone *unexpected*," Janet replied, a look of worry still darkening her face. "Poor traveler."

Agnes quickly joined her in her sobered state. "Oh, I see what you mean." After a moment, she scoffed and said, "I'm off to bed. Good night."

Janet watched her fellow housemaid leave the room before she finally made her way to her own quarters.

With any luck, she wouldn't be seen by the caller. As for the driver, she wasn't sure how she felt.

She feared she would have some explaining to do on the morrow.

CHAPTER 8
A FIRST FOR HER

Back in his lordship's bedchamber

Although Patience was fairly sure she knew what Max had in mind when he had her remove his dressing gown and her chemise, she was entirely unprepared for what he actually did.

She let out a squeak when he lifted a knee and climbed over the top of her, straddling one of her legs as his head landed between her breasts. Her hands immediately went to either side of his head, her fingers spearing his brown hair as he kissed both breasts. Then he licked and kissed his way down the front of her body. "Max," she whispered in a gentle scold.

She giggled when his whiskers tickled the skin above her mons, and then inhaled sharply when his hands slid along the back of her thighs until they were beneath her knees. He lifted them.

Settling his head between her thighs, he kissed and

supped on first one thigh and then another, nearly bruising the tender skin. When his tongue began teasing the folds protecting her womanhood, Patience held her breath. "What are you...?" She clamped her mouth shut when a sharp frisson of pleasure gripped her lower body. She couldn't help but jerk in his hold, which had his hands moving beneath the globes of her bottom to hold her in place.

"I take it your marquess never did this to you?" he whispered before his tongue once against sought its prey.

"Never," Patience managed in a hoarse whisper. She heard Max's chuckle and her eyes widened when she wondered what he was doing.

Whatever he was doing had the strangest sensations coursing about beneath her skin. A cascade of pleasures that were intense but not quite enough, each one building upon the last but leaving her in want of even more.

She wasn't sure what he did next, but she knew it had something to do with his lips and his tongue in her most private place, for the frissons seemed to merge all at once. A huge wave of pleasure had her gasping, had her back arching and her knees spreading wider. She might have even begged and pleaded and said a few incomprehensible words, but at no point did she tell him to stop nor did she scold him.

Still in the throes of the intense pleasure, Patience was aware of Max moving up and over her, of the length of his manhood sliding along her wet folds. Another round of frissons had her inhaling sharply. When the tip of his manhood nudged her entrance and then made its way into her, she inhaled again.

"Breathe, my sweet," Max ground out. "I don't want you fainting on me now." He pulled out nearly all the way and thrust into her, a growl from his throat making him sound like some sort of animal.

Well, he had captured his prey. Teased and toyed and tasted her, and now it seemed he wanted more.

Who was she to fight him off? Why would she even think to try? So she gripped the sides of his arms with her hands and held onto his thighs with her knees. His growls grew louder when his manhood settled into her more deeply with every thrust.

When his mouth lowered so he could kiss one of her nipples, she thrilled at the sensation, her chin lifting in response. His lips trailed to her other breast, and she let out a cry.

He had obviously been waiting for the response, for his movements quickened and then his body seized and his head lifted. For a moment, he looked as if he was being tortured. And then a moment later, he cursed softly as one of his arms bent. "Hold on tight," he whispered. Before he landed on Patience, he rolled onto his back but carried her with him so she ended up atop him.

"Oh!" she cried out, her head ending up in the

small of his shoulder and her knees on either side of his hips.

He chuckled despite his labored breathing. "Was that an 'oh' of satisfaction or an 'oh' of disappointment?"

Patience lifted her head to regard him a moment. "Satisfaction, of course," she replied in a whisper. "Is it always like that?"

He frowned and turn his head slightly. "Well, always, I should hope," he murmured. "Don't tell me you've never..." He allowed the sentence to trail off before he made a sound of disgust. "It's a wonder Billingsley ever got a child on you," he whispered. He tightened his hold on her for a moment before his body went lax and his breathing evened out.

Understanding then what he meant, Patience swallowed. A profound sense of disappointment settled over her when she realized what she could have had all the years she was married to the marquess.

If only she had rebelled! Argued with her father, or run away from home, or begged Max to kidnap her and take her to Gretna Green instead of doing her father's bidding and marrying the Marquess of Billingsley.

What a life the two of them might have had.

But I wouldn't have given birth to Thomas, she reasoned, tears pricking the corners of her eyes. There would have been a different son, though, maybe more than one. And daughters, too.

Would Max have turned into the grumpy, ornery

man he had become since she'd had to break off their betrothal? Or would he have enjoyed his life with her and their children? Surely his disposition would be better than it was now.

After a few minutes of introspection, Patience realized thinking of what might have been was fruitless. She was feeling boneless and weightless, a bit tired, and her backside was growing cold.

She pushed herself up enough to find the edge of the bed linens, pulling them up and over her until she was covered. When she attempted to roll off of Max's body, his arms tightened their hold on her and she was forced to settle her head back onto his chest.

Although it wasn't soft and round, it was still a good pillow.

CHAPTER 9
A SECOND FOR HIM

everal hours later

Max awoke with a start. Struggling to breathe, he discovered trying to sit up proved impossible.

His cock seemed content, however, given where it was still firmly lodged.

Patience stirred atop him, and he angled his head to see that she was right where he had left her when he had passed out.

The reminder of what he had done to her had his cock lengthening even more inside her, and he wondered how long it would be before she would sit up with a start and he could teach her how to ride St. George.

He grinned at the thought and marveled at how good it felt to wake up feeling something other than anger or regret, disappointment or depression.

How long had it been? He would have entertained the thought longer—and possibly sent himself back into his usual grumpy mood—except Patience stirred and mumbled something incomprehensible.

"What's that, my sweet?" he asked, his smile once again straining his cheek muscles.

Patience lifted her head from his chest, a look of confusion crossing her features. All at once, she seemed to remember where she was. "Am I crushing you?" she asked, about to attempt to move from atop him.

He chuckled. "Not at all," he replied, holding her firmly in place. If she was going anywhere, it would be to her knees. He had no intention of allowing her off his cockstand. "I'm actually quite comfortable."

Straightening, Patience did what his hold allowed in terms of sitting up. With her knees straddling his hips and her hands planted on his chest, she stared down at him in wonder.

"You're smiling," she whispered. Despite the fire having gone out in the fireplace, a lamp still burned somewhere else in the bedchamber. Since no light bled from the edges of the drapes, she knew it was still dark outside.

"You would be, too, if you were me and had a naked woman sitting on your cock," he replied as his hands moved behind his head and his fingers interlaced on the pillow. He looked rather proud of himself.

Patience arched a brow, about to counter his claim that she was naked. Noticing her chemise puddled at the edge of the bed, she gasped. Her arms quickly crossed over her bosom. "Max!"

He chuckled again, which had his body vibrating beneath hers. "God, but you're gorgeous, Patience," he said, moving his hands to rest on her hips.

Knowing he had already seen her—all of her—Patience lowered her hands to his chest. "I'll bet you say that to all the women who sit on top of you," she replied, curious as to how he would respond.

"All one of you," he countered, his smile fading to a wan grin. His eyes seemed to darken. "Will you ride me?"

She angled her head, wincing when she felt the simple bun on top of her head list to the side. From the strands of hair that hung from her temples, she knew her coiffure was nearly undone. "Are you sure I haven't already?" she asked as she lifted her hands to her hair and began pulling out the hairpins.

"I'm sure I would remember if you had," he commented drolly.

From the way Max watched her—lifting her arms had her breasts on full view—she wondered if he found her actions seductive. When one of his hands slid up the side of her torso and his thumb brushed over a nipple, she had her answer. She inhaled softly, well aware of how large his manhood had grown inside her. Of how her own body was responding to his, especially when she remembered the pleasures he had induced earlier.

When she had the last of the pins pulled from her hair and carefully held in a fist, she gave her head a shake. Raven tresses spilled down past her shoulders in waves.

She knew he liked what he saw, for she felt his reaction inside her. "Tell me what to do," she whispered.

Max didn't say a word, but he used his hands at her hips to lift her. Caught unawares, she tipped forward, her hands pressing into his chest to hold herself up. Once again, she felt his manhood react, and after a few experimental moves of lifting and lowering her hips, she knew what to do.

She also realized that if she did it too slowly, Max groaned. When she sped up her moves, his breathing increased and his limbs strained and the muscles in his arms bunched. When she knew she couldn't go any faster, she simply stayed with the rhythm they had established.

When he moved his thumbs to where their bodies met, a frisson of sharp pleasure had her gasping, and a moment later, she felt her body seem to come apart beneath her as wave upon wave of pleasure engulfed her. No longer able to keep her back straight, she slumped forward.

Max caught her before she crashed onto his chest. As he slowed her fall, she saw him wince and heard his subsequent groan as she felt a wash of warmth fill her.

Trembling from the exertion and from the frissons that continued to course through her body, Patience relaxed onto him, her knees still straddling his hips. She mewled as his arms settled around her back. "Are you all right?" she asked in a whisper.

Once again, Max's body seemed to vibrate beneath her as he chuckled. "I have never been better," he replied, amusement apparent in his voice.

"Oh, good," she murmured, relieved and rather proud she had been able to please him so.

Please herself, as well. She'd had no idea sexual congress could be so enjoyable.

"Just so you're aware, I'm not letting you out of this bed," Max said as he half-lifted her from his body so she could roll off of him.

She made a sound of protest when he pulled his manhood from her body, but she clung to the side of him—one arm atop his waist and a leg draped over one of his— once he was flat on his back again. Her head ended up in the small of his shoulder.

"Just so you're aware, I have a fist full of hairpins," she warned, gently pounding her fist against his chest.

"What do you intend to do with them?" he asked, imagining her using him as a pincushion. He couldn't help but grin at the ludicrous thought.

"Well, I shan't let go of them, or one of us may find ourselves impaled," she replied in a whisper.

"Give them to me now," he ordered, holding his open hand at his waist.

Patience dropped the wad of hairpins into his hand. "What are *you* going to do with them?"

He didn't answer but swung his arm out and dropped them onto the nightstand. "Save myself from a potential stabbing," he whispered. There was no humor in his voice, but he lifted his head to place a kiss on the top of hers.

He had already been hurt enough by the marchioness, and he had no intention of suffering any longer.

CHAPTER 10
A SURPRISE REUNION

The following morning

A loud *thump* followed by a startled curse had Jeffrey waking with a start. He turned his head to discover a young man dressed in a night shirt staring at him in horror.

"Who are you?"

Jeffrey rolled onto his side and lifted himself onto one elbow, resisting the urge to rub his eyes. The events of the night before came back in a flash, and he realized the teenager had to be the Higgins House stable boy, Hastings, who Mr. Cruthers had mentioned. The thump had no doubt occurred when the boy jumped down from the upper bunk. "Styles. The driver for the Marchioness of Billingsley," he replied. "Are you Hastings, by chance?"

The boy's eyes widened. "William, yes," he affirmed with a nod. "How long 'ave you been here?"

Jeffrey glanced around the loft. Although it wasn't as dark as when he'd turned down the flame on the coach lantern the night before, the sun hadn't yet risen. "Since about eight o'clock, I think it was." He smoothed a hand over his waistcoat pocket, relieved to feel the ring was still there.

"You musta been right quiet. I didn't hear you come in," William claimed.

Jeffrey remembered Mr. Cruthers' comment about the stable boy's ability to sleep through a thunderstorm and grinned. "I'm glad I didn't disturb you. Coach broke down near the end of the drive."

"Axle?" William asked with a wince.

"Wheel."

The boy waved a hand in dismissal. "You alone?"

Jeffrey moved his legs so he could sit up on the bed. "I was driving Lady Billingsley to Grayson Park."

His eyes rounding in shock, William looked as if he might faint. "What'd you do with 'er?" he asked as he glanced around the loft.

Wincing, Jeffrey hoped her ladyship was still alive. Hoped the Earl of Grump hadn't done something awful to her. "I left her with his lordship. At the main house," he replied. "Surely she was safe enough there." Afraid of what the stable boy might say in response, he decided it best to change the subject. "When is breakfast served?"

William blinked. "Uh, when the sun's about half up over the horizon," he replied. "Or when I'm done mucking the stalls, and watering the horses, and giving them their hay."

Jeffrey stood and stretched, his movements confined by the greatcoat he still wore. "There are two Cleveland bays down there," he commented. "I can see to them, but..." He raised a hand to his jaw and felt coarse whiskers. "I need to clean up and shave. Where—?"

"Through there," William said as he pointed to a door. "There's a privy of sorts, and Fields just brought up a pail of hot water. He's due with another any minute."

"Fields?"

"The footman."

"Ah. I left my valise on the coach," Jeffrey said, grimacing at the thought of having to go outside this early in the morning to retrieve it. The walk to the end of the drive and back would no doubt wake him up, but he was fairly sure it had snowed more after he had fallen asleep.

"You can use my razor," William offered. "I don't 'ave to use it much yet," he added as he smoothed a hand over his bare cheeks and grinned.

"That's very kind of you," Jeffrey said as he stood and stretched. He removed his greatcoat and glanced down his front. "Do I look like I slept in my clothes?"

William shrugged. "Who would notice?"

About to mention Janet Ludlow, Jeffrey decided it best he not say her name. "You have a point, although I need to be on my way to Kidderminster to find a wheelwright." He rolled up his sleeves.

"I'll have the cart hitched up after breakfast," William said. "Fields will be going to town anyway. He can take you."

"Much obliged," Jeffrey replied. He glanced around again. "Is Mr. Cruthers about?"

"Pro'bly with 'is wife," William replied as he pulled on a pair of socks.

"Wife?" Jeffrey repeated in surprise. Then he remembered what the groom had said the night before. That the cook was his wife. "Does she... live near here?"

"She has her quarters in the main house," Williams replied as he pulled on a pair of well-worn boots. "She's the cook, so he has coffee with her 'afore the sun rises and then stays for breakfast with all of us." He stomped his foot a couple of times to force it into its boot. "He keeps his bed up here. Says he likes the arrangement 'cuz he doesn't have to listen to her snorin'."

Jeffrey blinked. He couldn't imagine not wanting to sleep in the same bed as Janet. To hold her soft body against his, especially during the winter months. The few times he had done so, it had been after they had sneaked into her quarters at Grayson Park to kiss and quietly make love. He had hated having to leave her bed before dawn to return to his own. Hated to leave her behind when he'd had to drive the marquess or marchioness back to London, their only means of communication an occasional letter.

At least Lady Billingsley saw to it the postage was paid for letters that arrived for servants at the townhouse. If Janet had written to him since her move to Higgins House, the letter hadn't reached him prior to his departure for Grayson Park. He hoped she hadn't left her position there on account of him. Hoped she hadn't changed her mind about them. Although he had never actually proposed marriage, they had talked about it. She knew he had to earn enough before they could get married one day.

"I'm headin' down," William said after he had buttoned up his dark wool waistcoat.

"I'll be down shortly," Jeffrey replied as he headed to the privy. Surprised at the set up—a table with a pitcher and ewer, the pail of hot water still steaming, a small mirror hung on the wall, a large washtub, and a chamber pot—he quickly took advantage of the latter and set about making himself presentable.

As he shaved, he wondered what Janet's reaction would be to seeing him at breakfast. Would she grin and wink, as if to keep their relationship a secret? Or would she greet him openly and introduce him to the rest of the staff?

As he watered the horses, he practiced what he would say to her when he proposed marriage. Where would he do it? When would he do it? What might he say regarding their living situation?

Living four miles apart for the the next six months or so didn't seem like the best way to begin a marriage, but if that was their only option, he decided they could make it work.

As he made his way to the main house with William, his hair combed and his hands freshly washed, the scent of frying bacon wafted past his nostrils. He settled what he hoped was a pleasant expression on his face and stepped into the Higgins House kitchen.

The scullery maid was the first to notice him. "You must be Mr. Styles. Name's Annie. There's a place for you at the end of the table," she said as she motioned to one of nine place settings on a long wooden trestle. A young man—obviously the footman, Fields, given his height—an older woman who Hastings mentioned was the laundress, and Mr. Cruthers were already seated. "Help yourself to toast and jam. We'll serve the eggs as soon as the maids get down here." Annie resumed what she'd been doing, not giving him another look.

"Maids are always last to appear for breakfast," Mr. Cruthers said as Jeffrey took his seat. The groom had the place at the opposite end of the table from him. "They spend more time avoiding the possibility of runnin' into his lordship than they do cleaning."

"That is not the situation today," Bertram announced as he stepped into the kitchen from another door, followed by two women dressed in black and white livery. "His lordship is still abed."

A collective gasp from those who were already seated around the table had Jeffrey frowning. "Is Lord

Greenley usually awake this early?" From his time in London, he knew most aristocrats slept until mid-morning and some until well past noon.

The butler regarded him with a stern expression. "Indeed. And you would be?"

"Styles, sir. I'm Lady Billingsley's driver."

Bertram's eyes rounded, but only for a split second, quickly replaced by his usual expression of boredom. "Is her ladyship in residence at Grayson Park now?"

Jeffrey's gaze flicked to Janet. Dressed in a black gown, white apron, and white mob cap, she was staring at him as if she couldn't believe her eyes. "She's in residence *here*, sir. A wheel on her traveling coach broke near the end of the drive last night. Lord Greenley was... well, he was kind enough to offer us hospitality."

Well aware of all the eyes that turned to stare at him in disbelief, Jeffrey gave a shrug. "Well, he didn't turn us away," he added lamely.

Janet and the older maid, Agnes, turned to nervously stare at one another before settling their gazes back on Jeffrey. "But... but we was just in all the bedchambers upstairs," Agnes said, wringing her gnarled hands as her wide eyes filled with horror. "Openin' the drapes and, well... well, there was no one in any of the guest bedchambers—"

"Or the parlor or the library," Janet offered.

"What do you suppose he's done with her?" the older maid added in a worried whisper.

Janet's hands covered her mouth. "Poor Lady Billingsley. She was my mistress at Grayson Park. She was the kindest soul, too."

Bertram cleared his throat. Loudly. "I'm quite sure her ladyship is in no danger," he announced. "However, I will... I will confirm the situation momentarily." He moved to join Mrs. Cruthers at the stove. "It sounds as if chocolate will be required. Two cups, if you would," he said in a quiet voice.

The cook's eyes widened in delight. "Haven't made that in an age," she murmured in response, as if they were sharing a secret.

Bertram turned on his heel and walked between the two maids, apparently on his way to the second floor.

Jeffrey's gaze was on Janet as the two maids made their way to the table. When she was close enough to hear him, he whispered, "How do, Miss Ludlow? It's very good to see you again."

Janet inhaled softly. "And you, Mr. Styles," she replied, her head bobbing. "I don't think I've ever been so surprised in all my life," she claimed, although the shock of his presence wasn't as intense as it would have been if she hadn't paid witness to his arrival the night before. Otherwise, she was sure she would have fainted a moment ago.

"As was I, when I learned you worked here now." He didn't mean for the comment to sound as if he was scolding her, but he winced after he spoke. "Do you like it here?"

Janet's gaze immediately darted to Mr. Cruthers when she realized he had to have been the one to tell Jeffrey she had left Grayson Park. She took her seat at the trestle, her face displaying a pink blush along with a look of guilt. "I accepted the offer to work here when I saw the posting in Alveley," she explained. "It's a promotion of sorts for me."

"More pay, is what she really means," Agnes offered with a wink as she took her seat.

"You two know each other?" Mr. Cruthers asked as he leaned back to allow the scullery maid to place a plate of coddled eggs in front of him. The cook offered a platter of bacon to Fields and warned him not to eat all of it.

"Miss Ludlow and I have known each other for over five years," Jeffrey stated, not intending for his response to sound so defensive. Or possessive.

"Oh, have you now?" Mr. Cruthers countered, his brows waggling. "Are you intending to *do* something about it?"

Jeffrey furrowed his brows, aware everyone's attention was on him. "As a matter of fact, yes, sir, I am," he replied, his gaze darting to Janet. Her face still displayed a bright pink blush, and her eyes were as wide as they'd been when she first spotted him upon her arrival in the kitchen.

"You are?" she whispered. Her eyes seemed to widen even more.

He reached into his waistcoat pocket and pulled out

the ring. Gripping it between his thumb and forefinger, he held it up and then winced when he realized this was not the way he intended to make his intentions known.

"I am."

CHAPTER 11
MORNING BRINGS NEWS

eanwhile, on the second floor of Higgins House

A tentative knock on the bedchamber door had Max groaning. Unlike most mornings, he was warm and comfortable, his front tucked around a most glorious soft body, a curtain of silky black hair pressed into his chest. His knees were tucked behind bent limbs featuring smooth skin. One of his feet wasn't quite as warm as the rest of him, but he reasoned it was because there were no bed linens covering it. Tucking it under the covers would mean moving it, and he had no intention of doing so.

"What is it?" he called out, his voice raspy.

The door opened enough so Bertram could dare a glance inside. "My lord, there's a traveling coach at the end of the drive, but no one is inside..." He halted and blinked, his gaze having taken in the fact that there were two people in his master's bed.

"Give Fields some blunt and send him to Kidderminster. Tell him to take the cart. Coach needs a new wheel. And have him buy whatever Mrs. Cruthers needs for the pantry," Max ordered, not bothering to open his eyes.

He knew the knock had awakened the coach's owner, for she jerked in his hold but didn't try to escape. "Oh, and have her make a cup of chocolate for her ladyship."

There was a pause before the butler said anything, as if he was taking notes. "Yes, my lord," Bertram replied. "And your breakfast, sir?"

"In here," Max responded, managing to keep calm despite his growing irritation with the servant.

The door shut.

"My driver could have seen to it," Patience whispered. "He might have already set off to find a wheelwright." She turned her head in an attempt to make eye contact with the earl, but realized his head was above hers on the bed. "Thank you for ordering chocolate for me. I haven't had it in an age."

"I'm trying to be hospitable," Max murmured, tightening his hold on her.

Patience tittered. "You're doing an excellent job of it, darling. I don't think I've ever felt so warm on a winter morning in all my life."

He mumbled something, but sleep prevented him from finishing the thought.

Patience was wide awake, though, the events of the night before fresh in her mind. What he had done to her. What she had done to him. The pleasurable sensations she had experienced. She felt happy. Lighter than she had in years.

A hand went to her belly at the reminder that his seed was in her. For a moment, she couldn't decide if she liked the idea of carrying another child or not. If he had gotten a child on her, what would Max think about becoming a father again at his age? Could she even survive the child bed at her age?

She thought about where they were.

Higgins House.

Since it was so dark when she and Styles had approached the night before, she hadn't been able to take a good look at the outside. From what she had seen of the inside—the hall, staircases, one corridor and the master bedchamber—it seemed fairly well maintained. Not as elegant as Grayson Park, of course, but then that country house had benefitted from an excellent architect and a renowned decorator. The landscaping had been designed with a formal garden in the front and a pond and folly in the back.

But then there had been Max's claim that his bedchamber was the only one in Higgins House.

Surely the manor house had been built with eight

bedchambers or more. So what was wrong with the rest of them?

Patience was about to ask when Max let out a huff.

"What is it?" she asked, still unable to see him. She thought of rolling onto her front so she could face him, but it was rather comfortable tucked into the front of his body as she was. All warm and cozy, his heartbeat apparent behind her head.

"You're thoughts are rather loud," he grumbled.

About to turn over so she could see him, Patience instead froze in place. His words sounded gruff.

Was the grumpy earl back?

"My thoughts?" she repeated, wishing she could make out his mood.

"You're wide awake, aren't you?" he accused.

She inhaled softly. The grumpy earl was definitely back. "Yes," she admitted on a sigh.

There was a long pause before he asked, "Are you already thinking of leaving?"

Patience gave a start. "No." This time, she put the effort into turning over, although she kept her body close to his. "Did you want me to leave, Max?"

He opened one eye. "No," he groused. "Besides, you can't go until your coach is repaired." He swallowed. "So... what were you thinking?" Turning onto his side so he faced her, he wrapped an arm around her waist and pulled her closer.

Capturing her lower lip with an eye tooth, Patience wondered how to respond. She decided telling the truth would be the best. "I was thinking about last night. About how pleasurable it was, the way you made love to me and how I should have defied my father and made you take me to Scotland. And then I wondered if I was with child, what you would think if I was. And then I thought of Grayson Park and its gardens and how beautiful it is on the inside, and then I wondered about Higgins House, and why aren't there any other bedchambers besides this one?"

Max blinked as he stared at her. "You thought about all of that?" he asked in awe. "Just since you woke up?"

She nodded in the pillow. "What were you thinking?"

"About how much I need to piss," he replied with a huff.

It was Patience's turn to blink. "Max!" she scolded, but she soon grinned and tried hard to withhold a titter.

Despite his fierce expression, he chuckled. "Hold that thought, and try not to think too much. I'll be right back."

Max rolled onto his back and then onto his other side, cursing as he stepped from the bed. He grumbled about the cold and cursed again, this time more softly.

Patience watched as he made his way into the bathing chamber, grinning despite his suddenly foul mood.

Now that the room was lighter, she could better see

his body—the shape of his bottom, and the width of his thighs, and the size of his calves—and she would have continued to gaze at him but for what he said next.

"Quit gawking at my arse."

A hand moved to cover her mouth as Patience giggled. She couldn't help her amusement over his sullenness.

Perhaps he couldn't help himself. Perhaps it was his lot in life to be grumpy all the time.

Except she remembered his huge smile when she was atop him. How young he had looked. She was still grinning over the memory of it when he returned to the bed and hurriedly pulled the covers over his body. She let out a squeak at how chilled his skin felt despite how little time he had been out of the bed. "You're cold," she accused.

"I won't be for long if you stay right where you are," he replied, reestablishing the position he had been in prior to his departure from the bed. "What did I miss?"

Patience realized he was in a better mood and said, "I paid witness to the most amazing naked body a moment ago."

He scoffed. "The Greek god, you mean?"

"Yes."

When she didn't say anything else, he said, "I meant, what did you *think* about?"

"How do you know I thought about anything?" she asked, all innocence.

He gave her a quelling glance, and Patience sobered. "I remembered your smile, and I thought about how young it made you look," she said in a quiet voice. "Tell me, what would be required for you to display it more often?"

Any amusement he might have felt disappeared in an instant, and Max dropped his head onto the pillow.

Alarmed at the sudden change, Patience inhaled softly. "Oh, dear. I've offended you," she said, lifting herself onto an elbow. Her hand moved to rest on his bare chest.

He scoffed. "You have not, my lady. You've only reminded me of what I've become these past two decades," Max groused, his attention on the ceiling as one of his hands covered hers. "A giant troll who terrorizes the servants."

Patience scoffed. "I rather doubt describing yourself as a troll is appropriate. You're much too handsome, and I rather doubt a troll would have the body of a Greek god," she added.

His gaze darted to her. "You think so?"

She nodded. "I read many a fairy tale to my son when he was young," she claimed. "You're no troll." She rolled over onto her front and held herself up on her elbows. "How is it you haven't become soft in the middle?" Reaching over, she traced the muscles of his abdomen with a fingertip, which had him inhaling sharply. She quickly pulled her hand away, fearing what he might do to retaliate.

"You *want* me to be soft in the middle?"

Patience shook her head. "Of course not. Then you wouldn't have the body of a Greek god," she replied.

He smirked. "I ride a horse. Everyday," he stated.

"Is his name Pegasus?"

His grinned widened. "Thunder and Lightning. Neither one of them is capable of flying," he replied. "They're both Irish walkers."

"You ride *two* horses?" she asked, trying to imagine him mounted on more than one horse at the same time. "They must be terribly thin," she teased.

Max's head jerked in her direction, as if he almost believed she could think such a thing. When he saw her grin, he said, "One at a time, you minx."

She continued to grin as she watched him. "For how long?"

He shrugged in the pillow. "As long as it takes to go around a quarter of the earldom."

Patience furrowed a brow. "How large is the earldom?" she asked in awe.

"All the way around?" He paused to think on it. "The house is about in the middle, and I ride about eight or nine miles a day."

"That far?" she asked in surprise. "You must be gone for hours."

He nodded. "That's the idea. One day I head east to the border, go north to the border, go west halfway and then ride back home." He drew his route in the air as he spoke. "The next day, I go north, head west, go south halfway, and then come home, and so on." His finger continued to trace the path in the air before his hand fell onto his chest.

Using a fingernail, Patience traced his ride in the bed linen beneath her. "So, if you ride eight miles, then you would be going two to here, two to there, two to here and two back home," she murmured as a square indentation was left in the mattress. "Which means each of these outer borders is actually about four miles long. Is that right?"

He nodded. "Sounds about right," he agreed, "although two of those borders are a bit shorter—more like three miles because of the river and the canal." He rolled onto his side and used the tip of a finger to show her where the river bordered the earldom.

"I had no idea you had so much land," she murmured.

He moved his finger to her shoulder and traced a line along it, which sent a shiver through her arm. "Not a lot of farmland, of course," he said. At her questioning glance, he said, "A means for the land to make a living." He didn't add that there had been more of it at one time. Before his father's gambling had resulted in the loss of the unentailed properties.

"Ah. So what *do* you have?"

"Trees and sheep and a few villages. This house. Some other land in Staffordshire near where Barbara lives."

Patience rested her chin in her hand. "So when you ride, do you see people?"

He scoffed. "I try not to, but... I have to check in on the tenant farmers. I used to have a man of business do it, but he quit." When he noticed her arched brow, he added, "Don't ask."

"Max," she scolded softly.

"He wasn't doing the job, and I don't like paying a wage if a man's not actually working," he said in his own defense.

"That's fair," she replied.

He regarded her with a look of surprise for a moment before he settled onto his back.

"When do you usually go for your ride?" she asked, rolling onto her side so she could press her front against his left side. He wrapped an arm behind her shoulders and pulled her so she was more on top of him than not.

"I usually head out about now, but you're all soft and warm," he murmured, kissing the top of her head. "And I think it snowed again last night." He sighed, sounding content. "When I do go, would you ride with me?"

Patience gave a start. "I haven't ridden a horse in an age," she murmured.

"I would never have guessed it, given the way you rode me last night," he teased.

The reminder had her face warming with embarrassment. "I've certainly never ridden a horse astride," she whispered.

He kissed the top of her head. "There's a sidesaddle out in the stable," he offered.

"I don't have a riding habit with me," she countered, not sure she wanted to attempt a horseback ride. "I think there might be one at Grayson Park."

Max pulled her closer and he nuzzled her hair. "Well, I'd love to see you do an imitation of Lady Godiva, but it's far too cold for that today," he reasoned on a sigh.

"Even if it was warm, I wouldn't dare be caught without any clothes on. In fact," she started to push away from his body, but his arm gripped her tighter. "I was thinking I should get dressed."

"Not yet, Patience. Please stay where you are," he said.

Noting the pleading sound in his voice, Patience relaxed and settled her head back into the small of his shoulder. "With pleasure," she finally replied.

CHAPTER 12
A PROPOSAL GOES AWRY

*M*eanwhile, in the Higgins House kitchen
Are you intending to do something *about it?*

Mr. Cruthers' words repeated in Jeffrey's mind even as he wanted to crawl under the trestle and hide. Other than Janet Ludlow, he didn't know any of these people. Perhaps that helped, though, for he was determined he not look like a fool in front of the woman he wished to marry.

"I didn't mean for us to have an audience for this, but... Miss Janet Ludlow, will you do me the honor of becoming my wife?"

The collective gasp from all the servants seated around the trestle had the cook tittering as she set a bowl of beans in the middle of the table. "This has ta' be the oddest mornin' we've had in a long time," she whispered, her words directed to her husband. "Why, I haven't been asked to make chocolate in an age, and now this."

Cruthers furrowed a gray brow. "Chocolate?" he repeated before he remembered there was a marchioness in the house.

"And breakfast for *two*," she whispered.

His eyes widening in delight, Cruthers gave her a wink and turned his attention on Janet, as did everyone else at the table.

Janet blinked and looked as if she wanted to disappear as silence settled over the table. "You've caught me quite by surprise, Mr. Styles." She glanced around to discover everyone in the kitchen was staring at her. "Might I be allowed some time to think on it?" she asked in a meek voice.

The other servants scoffed and made sounds of protest in Jeffrey's favor while he stared at her in disbelief. "Surely you knew I was going to ask," he responded, the hurt in his voice apparent.

She shrugged. "Actually, I wasn't sure, since I so rarely see you," she replied in a quiet voice. "How was I to know? You might have taken a fancy to one of the maids at the Billingsley townhouse in Westminster," she added.

Jeffrey furrowed his brows. How could she think such a thing? They had kissed. They had made love. They had spoken of a future together. "Well, I haven't," he said in his own defense, attempting a pleasant expression. It was hard not to frown. Hard not to react with bitterness.

Except an image of the Earl of Greenley from the night before came to mind. He remembered how Max Higgins had gazed at Lady Billingsley, his face a mixture of rage and confusion and regret. He didn't want to look like that. He didn't want Janet thinking he was anything like the Earl of Grump.

When Jeffrey realized she was about to cry, he quickly capitulated. "But, yes, by all means. Do take some time to think on it. Perhaps later, after you've finished your work, we can discuss it. In private," he offered.

Bertram sniffed, his chin rising a notch. "She'll be available at two o'clock for one-half hour," he stated.

"I will?" Janet asked in surprise. Apparently it was a surprise to everyone else around the table, too, for they all turned to stare at Bertram in disbelief.

The butler gave her a quelling glance. "Might I suggest you meet in the parlor? I have reason to believe it will be unoccupied at that time."

Fields straightened in his chair, which made him the tallest at the table. "Isn't the parlor always unoccupied at two o'clock?" he asked before he displayed a look of bewilderment. "And pretty much all the rest of the time, too?"

Turning his attention to the footman, Bertram arched a brow. "Which is exactly why I mentioned it."

Jeffrey swallowed. "Mr. Fields, do you suppose we

can be back from Kidderminster by then?" he asked. He had no idea how long the footman's chores might take or if finding a wheelwright would be an easy task.

Apparently enjoying the attention, the footman seemed to give the query some thought before he nodded. "Why, yes, I do believe we can make it back by then."

"Two o'clock then," Jeffrey stated, his gaze going to Janet. "You'll be there?" From the way the others at the table hung on their every word, he was afraid they might all be in attendance as well, probably on the other side of the parlor door with their ears pressed against it.

He imagined pulling the door open and all of them losing their balance and falling onto the floor. Nearly chuckling at the thought, Jeffrey managed to suppress it with the memory of what had happened to Lady Billingsley when the front door had opened the night before and she had landed against the front of Lord Greenley. Jeffrey still didn't know if she had survived her encounter with the grouch, but he couldn't worry about that right then. Not with Janet's gaze on him.

She nodded her agreement and said, "I will meet you then," before she returned her attention to her plate.

Realizing there would be no answer to the marriage proposal over breakfast, the other servants turned their attentions to their meals and the morning small talk resumed.

CHAPTER 13
TERMS AND CONDITIONS

eanwhile, in the Higgins House master suite

"I wasn't always like this, you know." Despite his determination to shake off his latest depression, Max couldn't even manage a grin.

Patience leaned over and kissed his cheek. "I do know. I fondly remember our courtship. I think you were the happiest man in all of England," she said in a quiet voice.

"I was," he agreed, squeezing her hand.

She allowed a prim grin. "So what will it take to make you happy now?"

Max furrowed his brows, but more in thought rather than annoyance. "I need something to look forward to. Something to occupy my time that doesn't involve the earldom, or copying numbers into ledgers, or writing letters to people for whom I have little regard," he murmured.

"Oh, dear. Who might that be?"

He dipped his head. "Besides my man of business?" he asked rhetorically. "My sister."

Patience stared at him. "Beatrice or Barbara?" She had met both, of course, although she hadn't seen either one given both of them had left the capital before her come-out.

"Does it matter?" he replied and then rolled his eyes. "They're not so bad, really. It's just..." He sighed and then rubbed his face with his hands. "For two girls who had little or nothing in the way of dowries, and much to overcome due to father's faults, they both managed to marry very well," he remarked. "When I read their letters, I hear their written words as if they're speaking in my head, and I cannot help but think they're... they're bragging. That they are deliberately trying to hurt me."

"Max," Patience said softly. "They only want you to know that they've overcome your father," she said. "That despite how he treated them and how he left this world, they overcame it." She waited a moment before adding, "As did you."

He jerked his head in her direction and stared at her a moment before he finally nodded. "I cannot help but think that sometimes they think *I* am our father. That I am the same as him."

Despite the seriousness of his comment, Patience

tittered. "You are nothing like him," she said. "You're certainly more handsome. And he could never be mistaken for a Greek god."

He managed a chuckle before he sobered.

"So, you mentioned you needed something you could look forward to?" she prompted.

"Something to occupy my time. Something that won't disappoint me," he said, his gaze falling on her.

Patience jerked her head. "Touché," she murmured as she rolled her eyes, sure he meant her. Her arms crossed over her chest in an attempt to hide her nakedness. She knew she had hurt him. Badly. Perhaps he would never forgive her for having to marry Billingsley.

"I wasn't referring to you," he said, pulling one of her hands to his mouth so he could kiss her palm. He moved it to his chest.

"Then who else disappointed you?" she asked in confusion.

He sighed. "Not a who, but a... a *what*, I suppose."

It was Patience's turn to furrow her brows. "What's had you disappointed?"

"Me. My... my body, rather."

Giving him a look of disbelief, Patience allowed her gaze to travel over what she could see of him. "You're speaking of the body that could belong to a Greek god?" she asked, hoping she didn't sound as if she was teasing him. He seemed far too serious to be humored just then.

He nodded in the pillow. "The physician paid a call.

Bertram summoned him a few weeks ago because my heart was beating very fast, and I couldn't catch my breath, and, well, I—"

"Oh, my God," Patience whispered, her eyes rounding with worry. "What was wrong?"

Max shrugged. "Doctor couldn't say. By the time he got here, I was back to my normal grouchy self, and he left." He shrugged again.

She gave him a quelling glance. "Did you allow him to examine you?"

Looking ever so guilty, Max said, "Not exactly. I might have ordered him out of the house before he had much of a chance."

"Max!" she scolded. "He might have been able to determine what was wrong," she said on a sigh. "Heart palpitations are nothing to take lightly." After a moment, she displayed a look of confusion. "Wait. Is that why Marcus left Cambridge a fortnight ago?" she asked, remembering what her son had said about Marcus. "Thomas mentioned it when I accompanied him to board his ship a few days ago."

"Damn him," Max growled.

Patience gasped. "Max!"

"My son, not yours," he quickly clarified. "I told Marcus not to tell anyone."

Huffing, Patience said, "He didn't. Or at least, he didn't tell Thomas anything," she amended. "My son only noticed he'd left for a week but said Marcus had returned to classes. Before that, he was afraid Marcus had quit his studies."

The annoyance Max displayed seemed to abate some. "He didn't quit," Max stated. "He knows I'll have his hide if he doesn't graduate. He's my only heir."

Patience dipped her head. "Have you experienced any more episodes since that one time?" she asked, worry in her voice.

"No," he replied, although he hesitated before he said it.

"Would you tell me if you did?" she asked, suspicious.

"No."

Patience scoffed. She was about to scold him again when there was a knock at the door. She inhaled softly and dived under the covers before Max had a chance to call out, "Come."

The door opened to reveal Bertram carrying a breakfast tray. "Cups of chocolate and this morning's meal, my lord," he said, placing the tray on the night-stand. He was careful not to shove any of the hairpins onto the floor as he did so. "Cook will have more ready shortly."

"More?" Max repeated as he sat up part of the way in the bed.

"Mrs. Cruthers didn't know to make enough for two, sir, and Lady Billingsley's driver is eating with the servants."

"Hmph," Max responded as he made a shooing motion with his hand.

Bertram nodded and left, closing the door behind him.

"You can come out now," Max said as he pushed himself up to a sitting position and lifted the covers from over her head.

Patience emerged from the linens, her raven hair covering half her face, the ends curling around her breasts. When her gaze met his, she gave a start. "You're smiling," she said in awe.

"If you could see what I'm seeing, you would, too," he claimed. His eyes darted up. "Or maybe not." He chuckled. "God, you're gorgeous. You look like a wanton."

Pushing the hair from in front of her face, Patience inhaled softly. "So... would you smile like that every morning if I looked like this?" The thought of waking up every morning next to Max Higgins had a frisson darting through her middle.

"Probably."

She moved to sit next to him and then reached over to pick up the tray. She offered him a cup of chocolate since there were two on the tray.

He dared a suspicious glance into the cup before he took an experimental sip. He made a sound of appreciation and then added, "Most likely."

She took a sip of her chocolate. "Come for dinner at Grayson Park tonight and plan to spend the night as my guest," she suggested, her eyebrow arching. She doubted he would take her up on the invitation, but she wanted to see his reaction.

He frowned, ruining the pleasant expression he'd been displaying. "I've a better idea," he said as he helped himself to a piece of toast. "You stay here for dinner and spend the night."

Giggling, Patience was sure her face displayed a bright pink blush. "I may have to if Styles isn't able to replace the coach wheel," she murmured. "Are you quite sure you won't find me so vexing you'll wish me gone and take me to Grayson Park in your own coach?"

Finishing a forkful of eggs, he regarded her with a sideways glance. "Depends. How were you planning to vex me?" he asked, suspicious.

She finished her chocolate and set the cup aside. "I would never *plan* to vex you, Max. You must know I would never do anything to deliberately annoy you, but I can't help but think you're so used to living alone and being in a blue mood, that you cannot help but remain so."

He stared at her a moment, his expression growing serious. "You're saying there's no hope for me?"

Patience inhaled softly. The look of hurt on his face was there for an instant and then gone. "I suppose I'm asking if my presence would make you happy," she replied.

Max dipped his head, a piece of toast clutched in

one hand forgotten. "How long will you stay at Grayson Park?"

Allowing a shrug, Patience turned her attention to the food that remained on the plate. The single rasher of bacon was tempting, but she had lost her appetite. "I hadn't decided for certain, but I was thinking I would stay through the summer."

Giving a start, Max stared at her. "That long?"

She nodded. "Mayhap longer. Thomas will be on his Grand Tour for well beyond that. Probably two years, given the itinerary we agreed to," she explained. "I've grown tired of London. I thought to spend the rest of my mourning time at Grayson Park. Maybe take up drawing and painting again. Do some gardening."

Max stared at her for a moment, as if he was plotting something nefarious. "You can do that here," he offered.

Furrowing a brow in suspicion, she said, "I could. However," she waved to indicate the bedchamber, "you seem to be shy of space."

His mouth dropped open. "How much space do you need?"

She scoffed. "My own bedchamber, at the very least," she replied.

"You can have the one on the other side of the dressing room," he offered, pointing toward the door. "I'd rather you be close than on the other side of the house."

Patience couldn't help but grin at his offer. "A parlor... or a salon where I might—"

"I have one of those," he interrupted. "Both, in fact," he added, remembering the salon adjacent to the front door. "They're around here somewhere."

She tittered at the same moment a knock sounded at the door. Handing the plate of food to him, Patience scooted down under the covers at the same moment Max chuckled and called out, "Come!"

Once again, Bertram appeared with another tray of food. "Mrs. Cruthers finished the rest of your breakfast, sir," he said, pretending he didn't notice the lump under the bed covers. "Will you require anything else?" He switched out the first tray on the nightstand with a new one and waited for his master to reply.

Max's attention was on the lump in his bed. "Tell me, Bertram. Am I always a grouch?"

The butler seemed to think on the query for far too long before he said, "Not *always*, sir."

Frowning, Max challenged his servant. "Be honest. I won't fire you, if that's what you're concerned about."

Bertram raised two fingers to his temple, as if he was experiencing a slight headache. "No, sir, but you might act grumpier at some times than others if I am truthful."

"Bertram..." Max warned.

"Not always, sir. I do believe you were in good humor when I was here earlier this morning. Seeing your grin nearly had me fainting from shock," he remarked in a humorless voice. "And you were less grumpy than usual for most of the time your son was in residence recently."

"That much?" Max deadpanned.

Bertram ignored the comment. "You do seem to look forward to your daily horseback rides."

"I do, don't I?" Max murmured, his attention no longer on the butler.

"Indeed. Will there be anything else, sir?"

Max rested an arm on the lump next to him. "Are there still some maids in my employ? Or have I scared them all off?"

Bertram managed to maintain his look of boredom. "There are, sir. Two of them, since we hired Ludlow from Grayson Park." He pretended not to hear the gasp that emanated from under the covers.

Max certainly heard it, though, a grin lighting his face. "Well, that's a relief. Have them prepare the mistress suite for a guest. A permanent guest," he ordered, nearly grinning when he felt Patience's jerk beneath his arm. "And be sure the parlor is habitable."

The butler did his best to remain impassive. "It always is, sir," he replied, managing to keep a heavy sigh from sounding.

"Do we have a gardener?"

Bertram blinked. "It's winter, sir, so that would be a no."

"In the spring?" Max pressed.

Thinking his master was testing him, Bertram said,

"Mr. Cooper sees to the back gardens a couple of days a week when there's no snow. There's far more that could be done, of course, but you complained about the cost of having him here more often than twice a week."

Max ignored the jibe and asked, "Do we have a housekeeper?"

"We do not, sir."

"Hmph. Who does the menus? Orders the maids about?" He remembered his wife had seen to such details back when she was alive.

"The cook, sir." At his master's look of confusion, he added, "Mrs. Cruthers, sir."

"Ah," Max replied. "The one who doesn't allow me in the kitchens," he said, remembering the terms of her agreement to remain on staff. "Well, be sure she knows there will be two for dinner, and we've another servant to feed. A driver."

"Mr. Styles, you mean?" Bertram said, not bothering to remind the earl that the driver was already eating his breakfast downstairs.

"Him, yes."

"Very good. Will there be anything else, sir?"

Max thought for a moment and then shook his head. He managed a grin when he said, "That will be all."

His eyes rounding in shock, Bertram quickly took his leave, closing the door behind him so it nearly slammed.

Max was chuckling when Patience emerged from

beneath the covers, her expression nearly matching Bertram's. "You *pilfered* one of my maids from Grayson Park?" she accused.

Blinking, Max shook his head. "*I* didn't. Bertram did," he said, pointing towards the door. "Or rather, she left your employ of her own accord."

"Why is this the first I've heard of it?"

Max shrugged. "Hasn't been too long ago, I suppose. A month, maybe?"

An expression of worry crossed Patience's face. "I wonder why she left?"

"Probably because I pay her nearly double what she was making at Grayson House," he offered, obviously proud of it.

Patience wasn't impressed as she displayed an expression of sadness. "Poor Mr. Styles."

Max furrowed his brows. "Why do you say that?"

Sighing, Patience rolled her eyes. "I'm sure I'm not supposed to know, but he's sweet on Miss Ludlow, and I think she rather adores him," she explained. "He's been saving for years to buy her a ring. So they can be wed. But if they're not going to be working in the same household..." She allowed the sentence to trail off as she once again sighed.

A moment of introspection had Max slowly grinning until he chuckled out loud.

"What have *you* found so amusing?" she asked in annoyance.

"An obvious solution, of course," he murmured.

Rather than explaining himself, Max sat up straighter against the pillows. "Come here, you wanton widow," he said as he pulled her into his arms so she was sitting across his lap.

She gave a squeak at the unexpected move. "What are you doing?"

He used the palm of one hand to smooth her tousled hair away from her face. "This," he replied before he kissed her thoroughly. When he straightened, he stared up at her for a long time before he spoke. "Stay with me. If I prove too difficult to live with, then you can go to Grayson Park," he offered. "But don't be surprised if I show up there to bring you back."

"If I go to Grayson Park, would you come with me?"

An expression of pain crossed his face. "For how long?"

She inhaled softly. "Mayhap a few days. We could come back here for a few days. Or more," she suggested, noting he was actually giving it some thought.

"I suppose I could try," he hedged.

She lifted a hand to the side of his face, her thumbnail scraping his whiskers. "Are you sure?" she asked in a whisper.

He shook his head. "Not a bit. But I can't go on like this, Patience."

"Like what?"

"Behaving like a giant troll and terrorizing the servants with my grumpiness," he said.

"As long as you don't turn your ire on me," she warned before she kissed him on the corner of his mouth. "Because if you do, I *will* go to Grayson Park. Alone," she warned.

"It's all your fault," he countered.

"I know."

"Because I loved you."

"I know."

He stared at her for a moment. "Do you think you could ever love me back? Even if I am a grumpy old earl?"

She grinned and kissed him again. "Oh, Max, I have always loved you. I still do."

A slow smile spread over Max's face until he was fairly beaming in delight. "Damn, but my cheeks hurt with all this grinning," he complained.

She tittered. "That's because you don't do it enough, darling." Sobering, she said, "It's a wonder you can stand holding me this close."

"What do you mean?"

"I really must take a bath," she whispered. "Go for your ride. By the time you get back... what time do you usually return?"

He seemed to think on it a moment before he said, "Around two o'clock. Half-past sometimes."

"By that time, I'll have bathed and be dressed and

well into a good book. In that parlor you claim to have."

Max scoffed. "What makes you think I want you dressed?"

Patience regarded him with a prim grin. "You *are* determined I be a wanton," she accused.

His eyes darted to the side. "Maybe." He leaned over and planted a kiss on her forehead before he pushed himself off the bed. "Be sure to order tea for whilst you read your book," he suggested. "It will give Bertram something to do."

Patience scoffed. "I'm sure he has plenty to do, but tea does sound good on a cold winter day," she replied as she sneaked a passing glance at his retreating backside.

"Stop gawking at my arse," he called out before he disappeared into the bathing chamber.

By then, Patience's attention wasn't on his backside, though, but rather on the ceiling.

She had some thinking to do.

CHAPTER 14
A COUNTERPROPOSAL

ater, in the Higgins House master suite
When the mantel clock in the master suite chimed two times, Janet Ludlow froze.

"It's time you be gettin' ta' the parlor so as you can tell that nice Mr. Styles that you'll be marryin' 'im," Agnes said as she finished tucking in the bed linens. When she didn't hear a reply, she turned to discover Janet near tears. "Oh, now, what's this? There's no need to cry."

Sniffling, Janet said, "I don't know what to do." She shook the feather duster dangling from one hand, sending out a cloud of dust.

Agnes rolled her eyes. "Well, now that's what you'll be decidin' then, won't it?" she replied as she took the feather duster from Janet, captured her hand in one of hers, and led her down the corridor to the parlor. For a few steps, she actually had to pull Janet to get her legs to move. "Go on," she said as she shoved the younger housemaid into the oak-paneled room. "I'll finish up his lordship's bedchamber. Just have to sweep some toast crumbs outta the bed, is all."

The older maid disappeared down the corridor, and Janet turned to discover she wasn't alone in the parlor.

She expected Jeffrey to be present. Instead, Lady Billingsley regarded her from a chair near the fireplace, a cup of tea in one hand and a book held open in the other.

Intending to escape before her ladyship saw her, Janet was in the middle of turning around when she realized it was too late. The marchioness had already spotted her, the book she held now on her lap and her gaze filled with curiosity. "Oh, pardon me, my lady," Janet said in a pleading voice. "Bertram said the parlor would be unoccupied."

Patience angled her head as a slow smile appeared. "Miss Ludlow? Is that you?" When Janet nodded, curtsied and turned to leave, Patience quickly added, "Please, don't go."

Janet turned, her hands smoothing down her livery at her sides. "How do, my lady?" she said as she dipped another curtsy.

Setting aside her book and the cup of tea on the low table before her, Patience waved for the servant to join her. "Do come and take a seat. Have a cup of tea with me, won't you? I wish to speak with you."

Her eyes rounding at being invited to join her ladyship for tea—she wasn't sure if she was in for a scolding or merely an afternoon chat—Janet made her way to sit in the chair opposite of the marchioness. "I apologize for having left Grayson Park with only a week's notice, my lady."

"Apology accepted," Patience said as she finished pouring a cup of tea. She handed Janet the cup on a saucer. "Biscuit?" she asked as she lifted a plate of Dutch biscuits.

Never having taken tea with one of her betters before, Janet wasn't sure what to do. "Thank you, my lady." She helped herself to one, and when she noticed a biscuit rested on the marchioness' saucer, she placed hers on her saucer. Not sure what to do next, she simply waited, thinking she would copy whatever it was Lady Billingsley did.

"Since I didn't send for you, I expect you're to meet someone here at any moment?" Patience guessed.

Janet nodded. "Mr. Styles, yes. He, uh..." She sighed.

"Proposed?" Patience guessed, her eyes rounding slightly. She straightened in her chair, an expression of delight crossing her face. "Why, that's wonderful." When Janet didn't immediately respond, she added, "Is it not?"

"He had a gold ring," Janet said in a hoarse whisper. "Asked for my hand in front of everyone during breakfast this morning. I've never been so embarrassed in all my life." She took a gulp of tea.

Impressed that Jeffrey Styles would be brave enough to do such a thing, Patience said, "Oh, my. And what did you tell him, if I might be so bold as to ask?"

Janet seemed to deflate before her eyes. "I... I asked for time to think about it."

Patience retrieved her cup of tea from the table. "Which is perfectly reasonable," she replied.

"It is?"

Chuckling softly, Patience leaned forward and said, "I've known some young ladies who took *months* to give their answers, I suppose because they thought someone better might come along." She paused a moment, attempting to gauge the maid's reason for not giving Styles a response right away. "Do you suppose that might happen with you?"

Janet shook her head. "Oh, heavens, no. The only unmarried men in this household are Fields and Bertram, and I wouldn't be wantin' either one of them as a husband," she said, her body shuddering in disgust. "And other than the few men who work in service at Grayson Park, I really don't know any bachelors looking to marry," she explained. "All the servants seemed to think I should have given Mr. Styles an answer right then and there, but I hadn't even eaten my breakfast yet."

"Nor had your... coffee, I imagine," Patience guessed.

Janet gave her a watery grin. "Now that I'm not at Grayson Park, it doesn't seem as if marrying Mr. Styles would make for a very convenient situation. Not that I know what his salary is as your driver, but I make good blunt working here, so I don't wish to leave this position," she said. "Even if his lordship is a bit on the grumpy side, he's really no worse than Lord Billingsley was," she added. Her eyes suddenly rounded. "Oh, dear, my lady. I'm ever so sorry. That didn't come out right."

"Oh, I think it did," Patience countered, managing to suppress the wince she was about to display. Apparently her late husband's manner was as surly at Grayson Park as it was in London. "As for Mr. Styles' situation, I think I may have a solution that will work for both of you."

Janet's eyes rounded. "You do?"

At that moment, Jeffrey appeared on the threshold. His ragged breathing suggested he had climbed the stairs two at a time. "Forgive me, my sweet, but it took longer than we thought it would to find the wheelwright..." He paused halfway to where Patience and Janet were seated, his eyes widening in surprise. "Oh, pardon me, my lady," he said as he bowed.

"Oh, do join us, Mr. Styles. Now what was this you were saying about the wheelwright?" Patience asked, as she moved to pour another cup of tea.

Hat in hand, Jeffrey made his way to an adjacent settee and carefully lowered himself onto it. He accepted the cup of tea the marchioness offered, a Dutch biscuit already on the saucer. "Thank you, my lady," he replied, his eyes darting to see that Janet held a cup and saucer, too. "Uh, he's seeing to making a new wheel, and he thinks he'll have it ready day after tomorrow."

Patience considered the timeline. "That should work perfectly with our schedule," she said.

"It should?" he asked in surprise.

"Indeed. Now, I know you two have a topic of utmost importance to discuss, but I wish to make it clear that whatever you decide... well, please don't allow your concern about *where* you're working to determine your decision."

Jeffrey's brows furrowed in confusion. "My lady?" He glanced over at Janet.

"Pretend you'll be working in the same household," Patience clarified.

It was Janet's turn to say, "My lady?"

"Just... do what your heart tells you, won't you?" Patience set her cup down on the low table between her and Janet. "Because... because that's what I have to do. What I should have done many years ago."

Jeffrey blinked. "My lady?" he repeated. His eyes once again rounded. "Does this mean you're going to become the Countess of Grump?" He shook his head. "I meant the Countess of Greenley, of course."

Patience blinked as a brilliant smile lit her face. "Oh, my. I hadn't thought about it quite like that, but it does give me an idea," she said happily. She turned to Janet. "Ludlow, Baxter has retired, so it seems I am in need of a lady's maid. Do you think you would be up to the task?"

Janet's eyes rounded again. "Of course, my lady. I've even been styling Miss Sherman's hair on our days off. For practice, should an opportunity come about."

Patience grinned. "Good. You're hired. If you'll pardon me, I'm off to the stable."

Jeffrey quickly stood and bowed as the marchioness took her leave of the parlor, closing the door on her way out. He glanced over at Janet and at the empty chair across from her. "May I?" he asked.

"Please do," Janet murmured as she stared at the opposite wall.

He took a seat and placed his tea cup and saucer on the table. About to say something—he'd been rehearsing what to say whilst on the ride back from Kidderminster—he couldn't when Janet leaned forward and said, "I accept."

Blinking, Jeffrey said, "The offer to be a lady's maid?"

"Your offer of marriage," she clarified. "I accept. And I apologize for not having given you an answer over breakfast this morning, and it's not because I thought I was going to receive a better offer from someone else, because I don't, but because, well—"

"You didn't wish to be married and live apart," he finished for her.

She reluctantly nodded. "Something like that."

Jeffrey angled his head to one side. "I don't blame

you. Even if you still worked at Grayson Park, we wouldn't be together all the time. Her ladyship would no doubt go back to London on occasion. Mayhap for an entire Season," he reasoned. "But I decided long ago that I wanted you to be my wife even if I only got to see you a few *weeks* every year," he claimed. "For those weeks would be the most special of all my life. They have been."

Janet dipped her head. "We certainly wouldn't have tired of one another."

He scoffed. "There was that," he agreed. "Now... it sounds as if her ladyship will become the mistress of this house, and you'll be her lady's maid," he said as his grin widened.

"Indeed. Higgins House could definitely use a woman's touch," Janet said brightly. "Mrs. Cruthers sees to that sort of thing now, because his lordship doesn't have a wife or a housekeeper," she explained. "But Lady Billingsley will be so much better for this household. For his lordship," she added. "Oh, Jeffrey. This will be a perfect situation for the both of us."

Jeffrey stood and offered a hand to Janet to help her up. When she was standing, he kissed her on the lips and left his forehead pressed against hers. "I do hope the Earl and Countess of Grump are going to require a driver," he whispered.

Janet giggled. "If they don't, I probably make enough blunt for the both of us," she teased.

"You minx," he accused before he kissed her quite thoroughly.

They might have continued kissing but for the loud clearing of a throat that sounded from the parlor threshold. Quickly separating from one another, they turned to face the door and discovered Bertram regarding them with an impassive expression.

"I do hope you have solved your issue?" he asked in his bored baritone.

Glancing at one another, they both smiled and nodded. "In more ways than you can imagine," Jeffery replied.

CHAPTER 15
COMPROMISES

A *few minutes later, in the Higgins House stable*
When Max emerged from his horse's stall, where the Irish walker was happily dining on a forkful of hay, he turned to discover Patience watching him from inside the door. She still wore the widows' weeds she had been wearing the day before, and despite the winter chill in the air, she wore only a woolen shawl around her shoulders.

"This is a surprise," Max said as he removed his hat and pulled his leather gloves from his hands. "Do I dare ask what you're about?" A grin tugged at his lips, making him appear far younger than his forty-seven years.

"Hello, Max. How was the ride?" Patience asked, hoping his good mood would endure a few minutes longer.

He inhaled slowly, his gaze filled with suspicion.

"Surprisingly good, considering the snow that fell last night. The sun has made an appearance, though, and it's already melting." Frowning as he approached her, his perusal of her took in her bombazine gown. "Black does not look good on you," he added.

"I'm well aware," she replied as she managed to withhold a scold. "However, my trunks are still on the coach, and although your footman has returned from Kidderminster, I didn't think it my place to ask him to bring them in."

Max's eyes widened. "Does that mean you're spending the night with me?"

Patience dipped her head. "The wheelwright may not have a new wheel ready until the day after next, so might I continue to prevail upon your hospitality at least until then?" she asked before biting her lip.

His grin widening, Max said, "Of course, Patience." Glancing behind him to discover Hastings seeing to the other horses, he lowered his voice and added, "What about accepting my hospitality for longer than that? You're more than welcome, you must know."

Inhaling softly, Patience stepped forward so their fronts were nearly touching. "Would my driver be welcome to stay, as well?"

Max furrowed his brows. "Should I be jealous of Styles?" he asked, even more suspicious than before.

She scoffed as she wrapped the shawl tighter around her shoulders. "Of course not. He and your new housemaid Ludlow are betrothed." After a slight pause, she added, "The one you pilfered from me."

Glancing about the stable as if he was in search of something or someone, he returned his attention to Patience and asked, "Were they betrothed *before* your arrival?"

She shook her head. "He proposed at breakfast this morning. Ludlow gave him her answer a few minutes ago."

Max scoffed and retrieved his pocket watch from his waistcoat. He gave it a quick glance. "I've only been gone about four hours," he complained. "And your driver has already swooped in and captured the heart of one of my servants?" he asked in disbelief. "I suppose he's going to take her away from Higgins House once the coach wheel is replaced?" he guessed, his manner turning surly.

Her eyes darting to the side, Patience said, "Well, that all depends. You see, I asked Miss Ludlow if she would be my lady's maid, seeing as how I no longer have one, and she would very much like to accept the position."

His eyes rounding, Max huffed. "You're pilfering one of my servants?"

Patience winced at his use of the same claim she had used on him earlier that morning. "In a manner of speaking," she admitted. For a brief moment, she was sure a hint of amusement appeared in his expression, as if he was teasing her with his accusation. Emboldened by the thought, she squared her shoulders and inhaled. "Max, will you marry me?" She held her breath until she added, "I apologize. I don't have a betrothal ring I can give you right now, but I'm quite sure I can find something appropriate when I next go to town."

Max blinked. He blinked again. "Did you just propose marriage to me?"

She nodded. "I did." Her expectant expression lost a bit of its light the longer Max stared at her. "Did I… did I get it wrong? Oh, please say something, Max," she whispered. "Have I misjudged the situation?" she asked. "Am I a prize idiot?"

"To want to marry me?" he countered. "Absolutely," he stated. "But apparently, great minds really do think alike." He pulled a small box from his coat pocket. "Patience, will you marry me?" he asked as he opened the hinged box.

Patience gasped at seeing a ruby gemstone mounted on a gold ring resting in the black velvet box. "Max! Oh, it's gorgeous," she whispered. She looked up from the ring and asked, "Do you carry this around on your person all the time? In the event you're of a mind to propose marriage to someone?"

He threw back his head and chuckled. "No. Instead of taking my usual tour around the earldom, I rode to Kidderminster today. Bought it there at the goldsmith's shop, right after I bribed the wheelwright to take as much time as possible to make the new wheel for your coach."

Gasping, Patience stared at him as her expression changed from surprise to annoyance. "Max, you brute!" she scolded before a brilliant smile finally lit her face once again. She stood on tiptoe and kissed him on the corner of his mouth. "I do love you," she claimed.

He angled his head to one side. "I know. Apparently enough to marry me?" he countered.

"Yes, of cour..."

Max had her pulled into his arms and his lips on hers before she could finish her reply. At the sound of her slight moan, he deepened the kiss and knew the moment Hastings paid witness when he heard the stable boy gasp and the pitchfork fall to the ground.

At the sound of the gasp, a startled Patience quickly pulled away and glanced around Max to find the servant staring at them in disbelief.

Max's gaze darted over his shoulder. "Go to the kitchens, Hastings. Get yourself a cup of salop and a biscuit," he ordered, displaying a grin.

Hastings blinked. He blinked again before he tipped his cap and said, "Yes, my lord." He hurried out of the stable, managing a quick bow as he passed Patience.

She stared up at Max, her face pink with the embarrassment of being caught kissing by a stable boy. "I wonder what he's going to tell the cook?" she whispered.

Max seemed to think on the query for only a moment before he said, "Whatever he tells her, my reputation is ruined," he groused before another grin appeared. He kissed her again, his arms wrapping around her shoulders to pull her hard against the front of his body. Using the tip of his tongue, he separated her lips. A moment later, their tongues were tangling, and he was tasting her. Tasting the tea and biscuits she'd had in the parlor. Teasing her teeth with the tip of his tongue. Using his teeth to gently worry the pillow of her bottom lip.

When he finally came up for air, he stared down at her for a moment before he murmured, "I don't think I've felt this good in my entire life."

Rather dazed by the kiss, Patience blinked. "You were rather happy after we made love last night," she reminded him in a quiet whisper.

His grin widened. "I was, wasn't I?"

"You seemed even happier after you taught me how to ride St. George."

A chuckle erupted before Max began laughing. "Here I thought I dreamt that," he replied.

Her eyes widening in surprise, Patience tittered and placed her head in the small of his shoulder. "I look forward to making you happy for all the rest of your days, Maxwell Marcus Michael Matthew Higgins."

Max snorted as a grimace appeared. "My cheeks are going to hurt like hell, aren't they?"

Her titter turning into a giggle, Patience wrapped her arms around his neck and kissed him again. "You'll get used to it, darling."

CHAPTER 16
THE END IS MERELY THE BEGINNING

A few days later in the Higgins House parlor
"I heard the wheelwright arrived this morning," Janet said when Jeffrey joined her in the parlor. He was breathing heavily, having climbed the stairs two at a time after receiving a note that she wished to see him.

"He did. He fixed the wheel and the coach is now parked in the stable," he replied. "I received your note from Fields to meet you. Are you quite sure it's all right for us to be in here?" he asked, nervously glancing about before he closed the door. He rushed to embrace her and bussed her on the cheek.

"It is," she replied. "Her ladyship has gone to the earl's study. I expect she'll be there awhile, given how she's dressed," Janet said. One of her brows arched beneath her mob cap.

Jeffrey frowned but didn't press her for more details.

"Bertram tried to bribe the wheelwright to delay the repair, but the man wasn't havin' any of it. Claimed he didn't want the Earl of Grump angry at him, seein' as how he'd already accepted a bribe from him a few days ago to have the work done today."

Janet nodded her understanding. Having heard the tale of his lordship's ride to Kidderminster from the marchioness, she had kept the details of the earl's arrangement a secret from the other servants. They were already buzzing about how Lady Billingsley had apparently tamed the grouch that was his lordship and were wondering how she could be compelled to remain in residence. "I suppose this means we'll be heading off to Grayson Park soon?"

Screwing up his face, Jeffrey shrugged. "I haven't heard anything about that yet, but Bertram says I've been hired by his lordship. To drive him and her ladyship about," he said proudly. "And he gave me a raise in pay over what I was making working for Lord Billingsley."

Throwing her arms around his shoulders, Janet said, "Oh, that's wonderful news."

Jeffrey held her close and whispered, "I have even better news."

She pulled away. "You do?" Given the circumstances that led to their current situation, Janet couldn't believe their lives could get any better. They were due to marry in a fortnight, the banns having been read for the first time only the day before.

"Bertram says we can move into the largest of the servants' quarters," he claimed. "It has two beds and… well, it is larger than your current quarters." He had already sneaked into her room on two occasions late at night, once to simply kiss her goodnight and another to lie with her for a few hours. Although her cot was small, Janet hadn't minded. Jeffrey provided extra warmth her blankets couldn't.

"Maybe we could push the beds together," she suggested.

"That's an excellent idea," he agreed. "I already saw to it."

Janet giggled as she blushed a bright red. Remembering how she and Agnes had stared out the window of that room only the week before, she dipped her head. "It has a perfect vantage of the stable," she said.

He frowned. "Have you been watching someone from up there?" he asked in a suspicious voice.

She used the tip of her forefinger and pushed on his midsection. "Maybe," she replied, arching a teasing brow.

"You minx." His brows furrowed as he considered when she might have spied him in the yard outside the stable. "Did you see me? The night of my arrival?"

Nodding, she decided she could tell him the truth. "Agnes heard the commotion and had me join her," she explained. "I wasn't positive it was you—it was dark, and I was four stories up—but I hoped it was you."

Touched by her words, Jeffrey captured her lips

with his and kissed her quite thoroughly. When he pulled away, he left his forehead pressed against hers. "When we do go to Grayson Park, will you ride with me up on the bench?" he asked.

Her eyes rounded. "I'll have to. I've no intention of being in the coach with her ladyship and the earl."

Jeffrey frowned. "Why ever not?"

Janet gave him a quelling glance. "There are some things you can never put out of your mind's eye," she whispered. "And I refuse to imagine what they might do to one another when they're in the confines of the coach in private."

His brows still furrowed, Jeffrey said, "It's only four miles to Grayson Park," he reasoned. "What can they possibly do to one another in a half-hour? And in such a small space?"

Grinning, Janet whispered, "The inside of that coach is larger than my cot."

Jeffrey gave a start. "Oh. I see what you mean," he responded, a slow smile lighting his face. He kissed her before he could imagine anything else but the two of them wed and sharing a double-wide cot.

*M*eanwhile, down in the study
Having once again enjoyed breakfast in bed with Patience Seward Grayson, Max decided to delay his usual horseback ride until later in the day in favor of seeing to his correspondence.

He had never before noticed how much better the light was in the study in the early hours of a day. Never noticed how the dust motes danced about in the sunlight that streamed in from the room's only window. Never noticed how much more elegant the oak paneling appeared in daylight. Never noticed the elaborate patterns and rich colors in the thick Turkish carpeting. Never knew it was warmer in the morning than when he usually occupied the space that had become his refuge and his gaol in the evenings.

Well, evenings were going to be different now. Dinners weren't going to be quiet, lonely affairs. He could partake in a glass of port with his bride-to-be as she enjoyed tea in the parlor. He could read books next to the fire whilst he held her on his lap. When he was finished reading, he could simply turn his attention on her and enjoy a few minutes of kissing and quiet conversation before carrying her to his bedchamber.

Or hers. The mistress suite was rather beautiful, and the bed was at least as comfortable as his own.

He didn't really care where they slept or that it cost a bit more to heat another bedchamber. As long as Patience was in the same bed as he was, he found he slept better, especially after they made love.

Breakfasts were already better, and not only because Patience accommodated his request that she remain naked as they enjoyed their rashers of bacon and coddled eggs, buttered toast and cups of chocolate.

The toast crumbs in the bed linens were annoying,

but the housemaids had been apprised of the problem and would see to their removal each day. He'd had to hire another away from Grayson Park to replace Ludlow, now that she was Patience's lady's maid, but he wasn't about to tell Patience. With any luck, she wouldn't recognize the new maid.

All in all, life with Patience was proving quite satisfactory.

Max grinned as he pulled a sheet of stationery from the desk and then noticed he hadn't finished the letter he had started to write to Marcus the night of his betrothed's arrival.

Dipping his pen into the ink pot, his grin widened as he considered how different this letter would be than the one he intended to write.

Dear Marcus,

I apologize if you ever thought I complained about having fathered you. I was thrilled when you were born and am proud to call you my son. You'll make an excellent earl one day.

I write to you with a light heart and happy news.

I'll wait a moment as you pick yourself up off the floor, where you've no doubt landed after reading that last line.

I was remiss in never telling you why it was I have always been a grumpy old man—at least since you've known me, which is all your life, I suppose.

You see, a year before I married your sweet, sweet

mother (and a year before I had even met her, God rest her soul), I was planning to wed Lady Patience Seward, the youngest daughter of the Earl of Eversham.

Her father had other plans, however—he had betrothed her to Billingsley and hadn't bothered to inform her—but I wrongly assumed she had thrown me over. My initial disappointment slowly festered into bitterness, although your mother was a balm for the time we were together.

You have no doubt heard tales that she died deliberately just so she wouldn't have to abide my grouchy countenance. I can assure you, I was never a grump (or rarely, at least) in the company of your mother.

Now for the reason for my light heart.

Billingsley has left this earth and is no doubt in hell. Good riddance. (Yes, it makes me grouchy to think of him.)

Patience is now a widow.

Through a slight misfortune which turned out to be fortunate for me, and I suppose for her, I have secured her promise of marriage and have agreed to live part of the time at Grayson House and part of the time here at Higgins House when my presence isn't required in London.

Now for the happy news.

I have decided you should go on a Grand Tour. (I do hope you didn't end up back on the floor upon reading that last line. I shouldn't wish for you to be injured. You are my only heir, after all.)

*When you have completed your studies, we shall see
to it you can join your fellow heirs on a trek to Greece
and the Kingdom of the Two Sicilies.*

Do pick up your jaw from the floor.

I await your next letter.

Sincerely,

Father

*Postscriptum: If I've not said it lately, please know
that I love you, and I look forward to your return. If
you don't find me at Higgins House, I'll be at Grayson
Park.*

Max reread his scribbles, smiling at his attempts at humor. He had no idea how Marcus would react to his news, but he hoped the young man wouldn't think it necessary he be remanded to Bedlam.

He felt a hand on his shoulder and looked up to discover his betrothed was grinning.

"You do know that when Marcus reads this, he will think you a candidate for Bedlam," Patience said as she moved to rest a hip against the edge of the desk. She was dressed in a simple teal day gown, which high-lighted her aquamarine eyes and was the darkest colored frock she owned besides the few mourning gowns hanging in her wardrobe.

Max rolled his eyes, once again reminded of their like minds. "I was thinking the very same," he said before pulling her onto his lap. "What else should I be thinking?"

"That I might join you on a ride before you head off on your horseback ride," she replied, an elegant eyebrow arching. The weather had turned fine, and there was a perfect bench in the formal garden where they might enjoy a midday tryst. Still, it was a bit chilly out-of-doors.

Grinning, Max narrowed his eyes before he asked, "Did you find a riding habit?" he asked.

Wincing, Patience said, "I'm wearing it," she whispered. "With nothing underneath," she added, her mouth moving closer to his ear so she could capture his lobe between her lips and teeth. She felt his cock harden against her thigh, only the fabric of his pantaloons and her gown separating them.

He inhaled sharply, suddenly realizing her intention. "Am I to be your noble steed?"

Patience scoffed. "Well I didn't have anyone else in mind," she replied on a huff.

"That's a relief," he murmured, failing at suppressing a grin. "And where might this ride take place, my lady?" He moved a hand to the hem of her gown and slid it up to bare her calf and knee.

She gave a slight shrug. Although her gaze had moved to the room's only sofa, it scanned the rest of the study before settling on the very chair in which he sat.

"Why, I wouldn't even require a mounting block here," she replied.

Patience was about to step out of his hold so she

could stand, turn and straddle him, but Max had other ideas.

"I should like to warm up my rider first," he said as he angled her body so her back was pressed against his shoulder and chest. He lifted one of her legs so her slippered foot rested against the edge of the desk.

Patience let out a squeak at the sudden movement. "I thought *I* was supposed to warm up my mount."

"I wish to be sure she fully enjoys the ride," he went on, ignoring her look of alarm. He grasped the hem of her gown, already partway up her leg, and pulled it until her thighs were bare.

As Max nuzzled the side of her head with his nose and lips, his hand moved to cup her mound. Given her damp curls, he knew she was ready for him. Excitement at the thought that she had desired him even before she came into the study had his breathing quickening and his cock lengthening even more.

His middle finger slid through her honeyed folds, circled her womanhood, and dipped inside her. He continued circling the tip of it as Patience inhaled sharply. Her head fell back and her back arched as his thumb brushed over her womanhood.

Max knew the instant her ecstasy began. In the light from the room's only window, her features were exquisite, her long, black lashes resting on her cheeks as her lips parted and murmurs of 'Max' and 'yes' emanated from them.

When the hand holding her body against the front

of his moved to cup a breast, she cried out, and Max slowly ceased his other hand's ministrations. He drew his middle finger up through her curls, barely touching them until he reached the bare skin of her belly. Circling the tip there, he felt the frissons beneath her skin and thrilled at hearing her mewls and cries.

When she went limp in his arms, he kissed the side of her head.

"You wicked man," she murmured.

He scoffed. "A moment ago, I was your noble steed," he whispered.

She giggled, wriggled out of his hold, and turned to undo the fastening at the top of his pantaloons. "You wicked stallion," she amended.

Max watched in wonder, surprised she could recover so quickly. He finally assisted her in exposing his manhood, shocked as she deftly straddled him, pulling up on her skirts to keep them out of the way.

When she impaled herself on his cock, Max let out an 'oof' and wrapped his arms around her waist lest she fall backwards. "No mounting block needed indeed," he murmured in amusement. "This is going to be a short ride."

Her breathing still labored, Patience sat face to face with him, an impish grin lighting her face and her feet barely touching the floor. "Hello, Max," she whispered. She kissed him on the cheek as a blush colored her face. "You can trot now," she urged when he didn't respond. "Or would a canter be better for you?"

Amused, Max threw back his head and laughed. His entire body vibrated beneath hers, his manhood filling her to near bursting. "Or you could just bounce, my sweet," he said as he gripped her hips, lifted her slightly, and then pushed her down.

Understanding what she needed to do, Patience dug her toes into the carpeting for leverage and allowed him to set a rhythm. "This is hard," she whispered.

"Are you referring to my prick?"

"Well, that, too," she replied between her laboring breaths. "It would be easier if we were both naked."

The thought of her without any clothes on—in his study—in the light of day—had Max gulping. His ecstasy already imminent, he couldn't put voice to an answer as he pulled her close. His body seized, and his seed spilled into her. Groaning through his climax, he sounded as if he was in a great deal of pain. "Best ride I've ever had," he finally whispered as a grin lightened in his face. His eyes were closed, though, and for a moment, Patience thought he might have fallen asleep.

She stared down at him and then kissed the side of his head. "I feel as if I should offer you some oats or... or an apple," she murmured. "But I find I cannot."

"I am hungry," he whispered.

Patience relaxed into his hold. "We'll have luncheon," she offered. "And then you can go for your ride."

"All right," he agreed, his breathing finally returning to normal. "But we're doing his again."

Her eyes rounding, Patience said, "Now?"

His laughter filled the study, which had Patience slowly smiling. "Whenever you'd like," he replied. He regarded her with a wistful expression. "But first I shall make you my countess." His brows furrowed. "You do realize that by marrying me, you'll be the Countess of Greenley," he said quietly. "You won't mind the lesser title, I hope?"

She shook her head. "Countess of Grump is far better than Dowager Marchioness of Billingsley," she teased, "which is what I would become once Thomas sires an heir."

Max sighed, his grin still apparent. "Glad I can help."

Noting his continued amusement, Patience arched a brow as she drew a thumb along his. "You keep that up, and you'll lose your reputation as a grouch," she warned.

"I hopefully have, if Hastings has done what I think he has," he replied.

Patience stilled and stared at him. "What has he done?" She remembered Hastings had paid witness to their kiss in the stable. Poor boy had looked as if he was going to faint.

"Told the entire staff I gave him leave to drink salop and grinned at him."

Patience tittered. "If it helps, you definitely have Bertram flummoxed."

"Oh?" Max leaned back to regard her with a curious expression.

She nodded. "Mr. Styles spoke with me earlier today. When Bertram discovered the wheelwright had arrived to fix the coach this morning, he went out and was attempting to bribe the man to hold off on the repair until next week."

Max laughed, his hold on her tightening. "My sweet, Bertram wasn't doing it of his own accord," he said, a look of guilt crossing his face.

Her eyes rounding, Patience pounded his shoulder with a fist. "Max!" she scolded.

AUTHOR NOTES

Where did these characters come from?

If you are a regular reader of my *Aristocracy* series of books, you probably recognized a few of the characters mentioned in this book. For the story about Max's sister, Barbara Higgins Slater, you'll want to read *The Caress of a Commander*. Although Max is mentioned in that novel, this is the only story featuring him.

Oxford University Terms

The academic year starts on 1 October, and finishes on 30 September. There are three terms per year: Michaelmas (October—December), Lent (January—March) and Easter (April—June). Each teaching term (also known as Full Term) is eight weeks long.

Staffordshire's Border

Prior to 1895, Staffordshire included a C-shaped

"tail" at its southern borders with Worcester and Shropshire. This included the villages of Shatterford and Upper Arley, which were transferred to Worcestershire. Higgins House is located in that tail.

Your Invitation!

Do you crave historical romance filled with passion and red hot chemistry?

Come join me and my author friends in the Facebook group, Historical Harlots, for exclusive giveaways, chats with amazing HistRom authors, raunchy shenanigans, and more! https://www.facebook.com/groups/2102138599813601

ABOUT THE AUTHOR

A self-described nerd and student of history, Linda Rae spent many years as a published technical writer specializing in 3D graphics workstations, software and 3D animation (her movie credits include SHREK and SHREK 2). Getting lost in the rabbit holes of research has resulted in historical romances set in the Regency-era as well as Ancient Greece.

A fan of action-adventure movies, she can frequently be found at the local cinema. Although she no longer has any tropical fish, she follows the San Jose Sharks and makes her home in Cody, Wyoming.

For more information:
www.lindaraesande.com
Sign up for Linda Rae's newsletter:
Regency Romance with a Twist
Follow Linda Rae's blog:
Regency Romance with a Twist

www.ingramcontent.com/pod-product-compliance
Lightning Source LLC
Chambersburg PA
CBHW031024190726
48286CB00003BA/1002